THE QUE

THE QUEST OF KADJI

Lin Carter

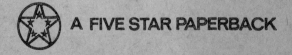 A FIVE STAR PAPERBACK

This edition published in MCMLXXIII by
PBS Limited, Victoria Mills, Pollard Street,
Manchester M4 7AU

Copyright © MCMLXXI by Lin Carter

Made and printed in Great Britain by
C. Nicholls & Company Ltd
The Philips Park Press, Manchester

The Quest of Kadji
is for that fine
Sword & Sorcery writer
MICHAEL MOORCOCK
my colleague in S.A.G.A.

The Contents of
THE QUEST OF KADJI

Prologue

ZAO, Olymbris, Thoorana, Zephrondus, and
   great Gulzund . . .
These are the five worlds that circle
The star Kylix in the constellation of the Unicorn.

And now of Gulzund would I speak.
No eye but mine has seen her whispering plains,
Her ebon cliffs, her dragon-guarded shores.

But I have voyaged thither in my dreams,
And watched the Red Hawk ride to the World's Edge,
And from my voyaging, bring back this tale . . .

Song of Worlds,
from
CHRONICLES OF KYLIX, the Fifth Book.

Part One

THE RED HAWK

The age is dark—the world is old—
The Gods are dead or gone away!
But what care we? For I am told
A man can die but once, they say!
—*Road Song of the Kozanga Nomads*

i. On the Great Plains

FOR THREE days and three nights the great clan of warriors had ridden without pause or rest across the worldwide plains of the whispering grasses, and in all that time no habitation of men had they seen.

But now, toward evening, one of the advance scouts turned back and rode like the very wind itself to the forefront of the weary and battle-stained legion. He rode up to the place where a tall bearded man, wrapped in a voluminous *ishlak* of striped red and black wool, bestrode a superb white stallion.

The scout swept his steed to a halt, hard wrists tightening on the reins, and flung himself from the saddle in a whirl of dust. He stood waiting for the grizzled leader of the war-stained host to ride up to where he stood, and when the white stallion neared, he seized its silver-studded bridle, snatched off his tall hat of red felt, and bowed his dark head.

"What is it, O Jorad? The foe, surely, are not before us, as they are close behind?"

"Nay, Lord—*huts!* A village; and—a well," said the scout.

The greybeard looked ahead, keen eyes narrowing, but the Great Plains ahead were dark with gathering dusk and even his eagle's gaze could not penetrate the limitless distances.

"How far, O Jorad?"

"An hour—two at the most, *jemadar.* Peasants. No horsemen, no fortifications, and the Dragon Banner"— here the young scout grimaced as if the phrase had a bad taste in his mouth, and spat in the dust at his feet— "the Dragon Banner flies neither from chieftain's post, nor lookout's nest, nor from atop the god house."

The bearded leader of the host grunted and frowned thoughtfully. To rest . . . even if for a little time . . . to dismount and to permit the stiffness to drain from taut and weary muscles . . . to ease chafed limbs and to forget for a time the endless rhythm of pounding hooves throbbing like drumbeats over the endless stretches of the plains . . . it was a delicious thought, and the promise was most tempting.

But was it wise? No man could say how close upon their heels followed the victorious and arrogant foe. It might well be that the pursuing enemy had given up and turned back days or hours since; it might also be that the legion had long since outdistanced the enemy, and could afford some hours of rest.

And it might also be that the village ahead, seemingly peaceful, was—a trap.

He sighed wearily, but from within; outwardly, no weariness or weakness or slightest sign of indecision was permitted to be visible in the stern, stiff mask of his face. And in the midst of his own exhaustion and suffering, and the perplexity of the present danger, and worryings about the hazards of the unknown future, he calmly and judiciously appraised their chances.

As if he read the mind of the *jemadar,* the young scout, Jorad, spoke up.

"Lord—I do not think it is a trap. The village lies alone in the empty plain. There is no place where the troops of the foe might hide."

The tall bearded man mused silently. He sat erect in the great saddle, stiff and tall as a spear, for all the pain of his wound. For three days since, when he and his men had been broken before the assault of the Rashemba knights at the battle of Agburz River, he had taken a lancehead in the shoulder. His sword arm was numb and useless, and despite the herbs bound to the wound, blood still trickled down his arm to splatter the tall dry grasses whereover they rode. The pain was very great, but his face was hard as iron and by no tremor in his voice nor wavering in his posture nor sign in his face did Zarouk, *jemadar* or Lord Chief of the fighting Kozanga Nomads betray the agony that tormented him.

"Very well; we shall make camp there. Surely we have put many leagues between the brethren and the accursed Rashemba by now. And the sword-brothers must rest. Ride thou ahead, O Jorad, and tell the villagers the Kozanga are coming—and that our needs are great!"

The young warrior grinned, white teeth flashing in the dusty mask of his face. Village camp meant hot meat and wine and a soft bed—*Hai-yaal* Gods! Almost had young Jorad forgotten the taste of wine and the feel of a bed beneath his weary bones!

He ducked his head, clapped the red felt cap back on his long black locks and turned to mount and ride when the *jemadar* spoke sharply, calling him back.

"And tell them, O Jorad, that we be the fighting Kozanga—true sons of the Great Plains—and no foreign dogs of Rashemba. We shall pay in red gold and white silver for food and drink and fodder. The Kozanga honor will take nothing at swordpoint from the people of the plains. Tell them that!"

The scout grinned and bobbed his dark head again.

"Aye, Lord!" Then he was off like the wind and the bearded Zarouk gazed after him wistfully. Ah, to be young and strong again, to fight all day and drink all night, and still be fresh to fight again the morrow! But he was old, old and grey, and his heart's blood was ebbing from him drop by drop through the red hole torn by the treacherous lancehead of a foreign dog of a Rashemba. Long had he led the clan of warriors; now, his days as *jemadar* were nearly at their end. Could he but live to shepherd the sword-brothers into the black mountains of Maroosh, where no man could follow, then could he rest content.

His wistful gaze hardened. His jaw muscles tightened under the crisp, iron-grey beard. Rest? Not while *one* man lived—the thrice-damned and god-accursed false princeling who had betrayed them to his foreign dog-friends . . .

Under his breath the gaunt old *jemadar* breathed five words—and whether it be a curse or a prayer, what man could say?

"Death to the Dragon Emperor!"

ii. *The Axe of Thom-Ra*

THE VILLAGE was a miserable cluster of log huts huddled together amidst the plain around an open square of beaten earth that the spring rains would turn to a sea of mud. But this was the beginning of winter, and although the snows had not yet come the earth was hard and dry and bare.

At the center of the bare space rose the village well. To the eastern side, rose the *go-mak*, the hut of the village chief. No less than the others of the small village, it was a squalid hovel, but taller than the rest and chinked with hard-packed clay. A feather-crested spear was thrust deep in the earth before its door. The red and gold feathers of the crest were old and tattered, faded and grey. Many generations had passed since the Ushamtar warriors who had come from the grasslands of the south to settle all this land had planted the proud war spear there as a rallying point. But the villagers were Ushamtar still, and they stood tall and proud and silent, with grave faces and keen eyes, arms folded on their chests, as the weary Nomad warriors entered the village with sundown.

By twos and threes the fighting Kozanga rode in, black moving shapes in the gathering gloom. The village chief had bade his wives build a great fire in the open space, and by its flickering red light the villagers could see the marks of battle on the torn and blood-stained *ishlaks* of the mounted men. Spired steel helms were dented; round leather-on-wicker shields were broken and battered; slim throwing spears were splintered. And many there were who did not ride but lay moaning in carts dragged behind the main body of the clan host, men with ravaged faces and haunted eyes, wrapped in filthy bandages.

The village women threw their hands up, clucking amongst themselves at the sight of the wounded warriors. And even before the Lord of the warrior legion had exchanged greetings with the village chief, they vanished into huts and reappeared with pots and jars of strong wine and basins of steaming water and packets of dried herbs and fresh bandages, torn perhaps from their voluminous underskirts, wherewith to treat the injured warriors.

Zarouk drew his great white stallion up before the *go-mak* of the chief with a flourish. With his left hand—for his right would serve him no more—he threw back the folds of his great *ishlak* and laid bare to the sight of men the glitter of the great hooked axe of cold steel he wore strapped to his girdle.

"*Hai-yaa!* The Peace of the Gods be with you, O Ushamtar!" he cried.

The village chieftain bowed low, touching the earth with the fingers of his right hand. "The fortune of Heaven ride with you, O Kozanga," he replied gravely.

For a moment they looked at each other thoughtfully, each fully conscious of the drama of the moment and each determined to uphold the honor and courtesy of their respective peoples. The villager was an old man, bony-shanked and bald of pate, his lean and leathery face seamed and wizened with the years. But his dark eyes were sharp and keen and watchful, and he stood proudly, his gaunt shoulders wrapped in a fringed *kuruz* of fine white cloth.

"Of your courtesy," the Lord said, "I require food and drink and a place to rest for my sword-brethren, and for our horses, fodder and shelter from the wolves and the night cold."

"All these shall be yours," the villager said. Zarouk paused, hesitant. Then, because honor demanded truth in full, he added:

"But I must declare that the Dragon Emperor of golden Khôr has named us rogues, outlaws and renegades, and set upon us his dogs, the foreign mercenaries of Rashemba, who may yet be to this hour on our trail. If you feel that our presence will bring danger upon your village, I say, speak out, and we will ride on . . ."

The face of the old chieftain did not change. Pride in his ancient blood and age-old heritage held him stiff with dignity.

He said; "I bow me in the shadow of the Lord of the Dragon Throne—a thousand years to his name!—I and my fathers have bowed to his shadow and we are his men. But, also, we are Ushamtar, and the great Kozanga warriors are our brethren from the days of old. I would spit on my grandfathers' bones, were I to deny hospitality to the sir-brethren of the Chayyim Kozanga. . . ."

The harsh lips of the *jemadar*, drawn thin and tight with weariness and suffering, twitched. But he said no word. With his left hand he drew the sacred Axe of Thom-Ra, the holy totem of the Kozanga, borne by a thousand *jemadars* of his race since Time's Dawn, and set it to his lips.

16

"The Peace be upon you all," he said, and permitted his *captains* to ease him down from the saddle, for he was too weak to dismount.

iii. Kozanga Vengeance!

FOR ONE night and no longer did the exhausted and beaten Nomads rest in the village of the Ushamtar. They ate and drank hugely, paying with red gold for the hospitality of their hosts, as was the ancient custom. Then, having seen their blown and weary horses fed, watered, rubbed down and in safe shelter—and then only—did the proud Kozanga sleep. Like dead men they slept, but woke with first light of dawn to move on. Ahead of them, many leagues across the endless plains of whispering grass, lay the black mountains. Impassable to any man but a Kozanga were those tall and mighty mountains of black stone—an impregnable fortress of dark stone, hewn by the very hands of the Gods at the dim, forgotten beginning of things.

The secret passage through that wall of black rock was the hereditary secret of the Kozanga swordbrethren, for ages ago the fathers of the Nomad warrior clan had first raised the red-and-black war standard of their legion behind those mountains, on the banks of Chaya, the Sacred River. For thousands of years the sons of the Chayyim Kozanga had passed that secret down the generations. Could they but reach that frowning rampart of black stone in the land of Maroosh, they would be safe—aye, and let the pursuing Rashemba knights yap like dogs at a closed gate! There, in the hidden valleys and the secret places of the mountains, the heroes of the conquered and broken legion could rest, heal their wounds, hone their blades, to ride again another day.

Aye! To ride straight to the tall gates of golden Khôr that had sold them to the foreign dogs! All of the Empire of the Dragon would feel that cold kiss of steel and taste the sour wine of fear when the mighty Kozanga brethren rode on the trail of vengeance! That the old *jemadar* swore, deep in his soul.

With first light he summoned to the hut wherein he lay his grandson, Kadji. He watched with proud eyes as the tall youth, wrapped in a flowing *ishlak* of tribal red and black, his blond locks flying free in the frosty air, rode up in a thunder of hooves before the hut and swung from the saddle to kneel in the dirt before his grandsire.

The grizzled Lord smiled slightly, and set one mighty hand on the boy's head, lifting his face. Like a young hawk, Kadji raised bright, fierce eyes to meet his gaze. Blue as heaven and bright as sword steel were those clear young eyes, fearless and keen. The face of the youth was fair, but not soft: strong and lean, tanned to the hue of old leather by sun and wind, with lips that smiled and laughed, but he had the strong square jaw of his fathers and the bright gold mane of his mother. *Kadji* he was named, which was "Red Hawk" in the tongue of the Great Plains. And like a hunting hawk could he hurtle across the measureless leagues of whispering grass, astride his black Feridoon pony.

A fine hunter was the boy, and a fierce swordsman, for all his young years. His steady nerve and bold daring and bright, mischievous ways had made him beloved among the sword-brethren of the Kozanga. And Zarouk knew, deep in his heart, that when he could no longer lead the charge, the elder brothers of the legion would pass the name of *jemadar* to Kadji the Red Hawk. . . .

"The Lord summoned me?" the boy demanded. Old Zarouk nodded.

18

"With full dawn, the sword-brethren ride, O Kadji! In the valleys of black rock, in the hidden places, there shall we rest. Beside the sacred banks of Mother Chaya shall we renew our strength, to rise and ride again and sweep the streets of traitorous Khôr with our bright swords. The dog-hearted knights of Rashemba shall we drive back to their foul kennels in the west, and they shall learn to tremble at the name of the Kozanga vengeance—aye, even they, who laugh now at the name!"

The boy nodded, eyes blazing. Unconsciously, he fell into the chanting, ceremonial rhythm of Zarouk's words.

"*Hai-yaa, jemadar!* Mother Chaya shall wash clean the wounds of her children of the plains, and Father Sky shall echo again to the thunder of our hooves, when the Kozanga ride to vengeance! We shall ride to the foot of the Dragon Throne and take our honor back at swordpoint from the hands of the Great Father, aye, from the hands of Holy Yakthodah shall we receive our honor!"

"*Nay!*"

Zarouk spoke like a great war trumpet and the boy Kadji blinked at the word.

"Speak, Lord!" he begged.

The eyes of Zarouk burned into the face of the boy.

"The sword-brothers shall ride into the hidden fast-nesses of the black mountains, aye, and mayhap the Red Tents shall rise again on the shores of Mother Chaya, but Kadji the Red Hawk shall not ride thither. Neither shall we take our honor back from the hands of Yakthodah the Holy Dragon Emperor—not while the world lasts!"

The boy did not understand his grandsire's words. His lips trembled and his blue eyes questioned, but he waited without asking. Zarouk drew a deep breath.

19

How to phrase it—how to lay the great task on these young shoulders?

"Listen to my words, O Kadji! Thou knowest that when the Dragon Emperor, Azakour, third of that name, died twenty years since, all of the Dragon Empire was thrown into turmoil and confusion for lack of a true-born heir?"

"Aye, Lord."

"For unto the Lord Azakour Third were but two sons born: the eldest, Hodaky, was sickly and died young, and the youngest, Yakthodah, died whilst on his foreign travels to the court of the High Prince of Rashemba. The Dragon Throne empty, with no living heir, no man knew who should wear the White Crown and rule sovereign over all the plains. And the noble lords, the *kugars,* the fat landowners, even they our old oppressors, traitorous and ambitious and cunning, they whom the Old Emperor had put down and banished— came they not riding back, to try their power one against the other, that the strongest of them all should seize the Khalidûr and take the name of Emperor? And was not all of the Empire of the Dragon torn asunder with civil war?"

"Aye, Lord!"

"Then came the miracle! Out of westerly Rashemba came word that the Prince Yakthodah lived! That assassins of the banished *kugars* had sought his life, but slew another thinking it was he—while the True Prince fled into hiding under a name not his. You were a child when this word first came to the plains. Like the wind of spring it was, and our hearts flowered with joy at its coming. And thence into the Empire rode the Prince, with a mighty host of the chivalry of Rashemba by his side, to drive out the usurpation of the *kugars* and to claim his holy father's throne. Did not the great Kozanga raise the war standard and ride by his side? Did not the sword-brothers of the Chayyim Kozanga break the *kugars* at the Hills of Yush? Did not I, Zarouk, stand in the Hall of Halls and see the True Prince crowned as Dragon Emperor? Did not he name me 'brother' and 'friend' before all men?"

"I swear that all these things are true," the boy said solemnly.

The old warrior heaved a sigh.

"*Aiii*, for the sword-brethren! For dark days came upon us soon after! The Dragon was not the man his father was! The wealth of his ancestors he squandered for gauds and baubles! The gold of Khôr he spent on jugglers and astrologers and magicians! Did he not spend his days in frivolity and his nights in gaming, drinking and revel? Did he not build his Dragon Guard—not from the sword-brothers of the plains—but from among the dog-knights of Rashemba? Did not he take as his Empress the foreign woman—the very daughter of the High Prince Bayazin who had lent him an army to whelm the *kugars*? And did he not, once the coffers were empty, welcome back the same *kugars* he had broken and banished—they and their gold? Did he not trade them Kozanga land for their gold? Did he not turn against us of the Kozanga, to curry favor with the *kugars* . . . did he not, at the last, outlaw and banish us, forbidding that a Chayyim Kozanga should enter the gates of golden Khôr? And then, as we rode from his lands with dignity, did he not loose upon our heels the dogs of Rashemba, to ambush and slaughter us? Which he would have done, had not the Gods warned us in time with the Omen of the Wolves . . ."

Kadji bent his head and beat his chest.

"Lord *jemadar*, alas, all these things are true!"

"Very well! Now, hearken thou, O Red Hawk, O son of my own son. In the darkness of night the War Prince of the Gods came to me in my dream and spake unto me, saying, behold, O Elder Brother of the Kozanga, the man that sits in the chair of Azakour *is not the son of his blood, but a vile and cunning impostor!"*

iv. *The Red Hawk Rides*

NOON FOUND the boy Kadji half a league from the village whereat the legion had slept the night before. Alone, mounted on his favorite Feridoon pony, the youth had retraced the path the Nomads had taken in their flight from the lances of Rashemba. Now the boy reined to a halt atop the brow of a low hill to scan the horizon. Were the knights of Prince Bayazin still on the track of the brethren, or had the dogs turned back to the Dragon City—back to golden Khôr where a foul deceiver ruled from the holy chair of a thousand Emperors? The boy cursed and spat at the thought.

The clear skies of noon shone down with a fierce light on the measureless plains below. Cold and frosty was the wind, with the touch of winter in it, but the sun burned hot and bright. Searching the horizon, Kadji found no trace of mounted warriors. No trail of dust rose to mark their wake, no burnished helm or shield caught and mirrored the brilliant noon. He decided to rest, to eat and drink, before riding on to continue the mighty mission the *jemadar* had laid upon his shoulders.

And, truly, the Quest laid upon him was a great one.

The War Prince of the Gods, even the same Divine Thom-Ra who had given the holy Axe to Kozang of Chaya, the father of his people, in ancient times, had declared the Dragon Emperor a cunning thief of crowns. No child of the dead Emperor was he, but a sly Perushka bastard—born to a tavern slut of Perushk and fathered by a renegade *kugar* lordling. With incredible boldness and guile the impostor, whose real name the God said was Shamad, had somehow convinced the monarch of Rashemba, Bayazin the High Prince, that his claim to the throne was true—and a war-weary land, torn by civil strife and yearning for the peaceful central rule of a Holy Dragon Emperor again, had welcomed the liar with open gates! Kadji ground his teeth at the thought.

Kozanga honor demanded that a high born warrior of the sword-brethren avenge both the insult to the Dragon Throne and the outrage against the Nomad legion by the death of this Shamad. The double deed had been bestowed upon the boy Kadji. His hand would wield the blade that cut the throat of Shamad the Pretender.

And the God-Axe itself would be that blade. For, lo, the sacred Axe of the Chayyim Kozanga hung glittering at Kadji's girdle!

The boy's heart was filled with grim purpose . . . but he was a boy, and not yet fully come to manhood. Hence, like all boys, he dreamed of high heroic deeds— of winning the applause of the sword-brothers with some glorious deed, some mighty accomplishment. And what higher deed than this could even Kadji have dreamed of? Thus in his young heart exultation beat high, and he thrilled in anticipation of the days to come.

As he sat cross-legged in the grass at the foot of the hill, chewing on dried meat and dates and sucking sour wine from a goatskin bag, he dreamed of the thing. Resplendent in his Kozanga *ishlak* of red and black stripes, the Axe naked in his strong right hand, he would stride fearlessly through the whispering ranks of fat, greasy-faced *kugar* lordlings. Straight up to the foot of the Dragon Throne he would stride with bold steps, head high, looking neither to the right nor the left. There, at the foot of the great dais, he would confront Shamad the Impostor and declare his crimes in the name of the

Most High Gods—the cry of Kozanga vengeance ringing on his lips, he would lift the ancient Axe—and the head of the false Dragon would roll in black and stinking gore at his feet, while the Dragon City thundered, as with one voice, the name of Kadji—Red Hawk of the Kozanga Nomads!

It was a beautiful dream, and sucking wine from the skin bag, the boy warrior of the Plains vowed he would make it come true. Aye, the Axe of Thom-Ra would drink the blood of Shamad even if Kadji had to follow the cowardly traitor to the very Edge of the World itself . . . aye, to the very gates of bright Ithombar, king city of the Immortals, whose purple towers rose on the world's remotest rim!

It was to be very many months before Kadji could know how prophetic was that vow. . . .

HE SLEPT that night upon the bosom of the Great Plains, using his saddle for a pillow as did Kozanga warriors. And with dawn he rode on, and thus for two days he retraced the flight of the Nomad legion until at last he was come to the bloody shores of the Agburz. Here, six days before, the honor of the Kozanga Nomads had been trampled before the pounding hooves of the Rashemba chivalry. He rested beside the river, thinking of the battle. Old Thugar had fallen in the onslaught, Thugar, who had taught him to use the great bow of the plains; aye, and clever, mocking Korak, his boyhood friend; and Horem, too, and that great horseman, Gomar of the White Lance . . . how many of the great hero-brethren had fallen before the ponderous stallions of the mailed knights of western Rashemba!

Kneeling in the trodden dust, the Red Hawk swore before his savage Gods the sword-brethren should not have died in vain.

24

He kissed the blade of the sacred Axe in token of his vow and rose and rode on, and his heart was filled with grim purpose. But now he must ride with very great care, scanning the world around from every hillcrest or elevation. It would seem that the dog-knights of Rashemba had turned back in truth from their pursuit of the clan legion, for he saw no sign of them as he retraced, day after day, the flight of the sword-brothers. But here, on the far shore of the Agburz, he was in the country held by the foe, and well might they have left guardposts or watch parties behind to warn against the return of the Chayyim Kozanga Nomads. So he rode carefully, muffled in his cloak, taking advantage of every bit of cover the landscape might afford. He followed the winding path of dry gullies; he picked his way through the stand of trees, using the bushy underbrush to hide him from any watchful eye; and thus he passed many leagues unseen by any man.

v. The Gates of Nabdoor

IT WAS some days later that Kadji, Red Hawk of the Chayyim Kozanga, came within sight of Nabdoor.

The small traders' town lay below him, for now he was among the Barren Hills, and the settlement lay below on the banks of the Babdar, a small river that wandered out of the north and down whose meandering stream came flatboats from the northern farms bearing goods to market. Here at this spot the river from the north met with the great caravan routes that crisscrossed the plains from east to west: hence a permanent village of tradesmen, artisans, caravan lords and merchant princelings had grown up in olden time.

Now it might well be that the Rashemba, turning back from the Field of Agburz to return to the heartlands of the Dragon Emperor, might have paused at Nabdoor-town. At very least, it seemed likely they had left a garrison to ward and hold this outpost of golden Khôr. Therefore the boy Kadji tethered his pony to dry brush below and wriggled on his belly to the hillcrest, from which high vantage he could gaze down and see the streets and ways of Nabdoor spread out below him like a living map. He searched with keen and thoughtful eyes and saw that his worst fears were realized; for while the main body of the Rashemba host had departed from these parts, a garrison did indeed hold the gates and walls of the town.

Kadji crawled down from the hillcrest to where his pony waited patiently and huddled in his robes, munched dry provisions while he thought out his strategy. The pony nosed him and he dug a handful of dry meal from the saddlebags and let it eat from the palm of his hand, chuckling as the moist, bristled lips moved over his hand.

"What shall we do, eh, Haral?" he murmured, stroking the velvet nose of the pony. "Of course, we could circle Nabdoor without entering it, and continue on into the north . . . but if we so do, little Haral, we shall both go with empty bellies many a day, for there is little left in the bags for you to feed upon, and naught at all for me."

The pony whickered softly and shoved his shoulder with its nose, as if to say "Let's go down and dare it."

At length Kadji made up his mind. His pony was of Feridoon breed, unlike the proud war stallions of the sword-brothers; and he himself, with his blond locks and blue eyes—a rarity in the Nomad clan-brethren—could pass for an Ushamtar of the plains. And he had cleverly bethought him of the time when perchance he might need to hide his Kozanga identity behind some manner of disguise; thus he bore with him in the saddle

26

pack garments purchased from the *go-n.* ....
Ushamtar village whereat they had paused to
night.

On sudden impulse the boy rose and threw off the
felt hat and striped *ishlak* robes, which would mark him
to all eyes as a warrior of the Chayyim Kozanga.

Nude save for a linen clout wound about his loins, the
boy stooped and bathed in the cold waters of the Babdar, which, like a mirror, caught and held the image of
his lean brown young body, broad-shouldered, smooth-
chested, narrow-hipped, and long and rangy in the legs.
He bent, grinning, and scooped cold water up in cupped
palms, slashing it in his face, shivering at the bite of
the chill water as it dribbled down his naked breast and
thighs.

When he had cleansed himself, he opened the saddle
pack and took out fresh garments, which he drew on
over his shivering nakedness.

In a few moments he wore the fringed *kuruz*, the
high-strapped leggings, the broad girdle and belled cap
of a lordless Free Sword of the Ushamtar. The Ushamtar warriors had taken no part in the battle between the
foreign Rashemba knights and the sword-brothers of
the Kozanga; no curse of banishment or outlawry lay on
their heads; thus, in the guise of a wandering Ushamtar
mercenary, Kadji could ride where he wished without
fear. He hoped!

Mounting his Feridoon pony, he rode boldly down to
the gates of Nabdoor.

The town, which was not large, was ringed about in
the embrace of a wall of rough fieldstone covered with
cream and white stucco. It had two gates fashioned of
heavy wood, and up to the nearer of these rode Kadji.
As a boy might, he had concocted a long and very complicated story to account for his presence here. It in-
cluded a false name and a full genealogy, and much in-

dental and anecdotal material. But to the vast disgust of Kadji, the knights of the Rashemba garrison did not even question him. Huge and red-faced and surly, they looked down at him from the height of the wall, saw him for a Ushamtar mercenary, and gestured him through the gate with but a grunted word. He felt somehow cheated: but it was just as well. His tongue might betray him for a Kozanga. He had not the guttural accents of a true born Ushamtar, although he had not thought of this.

He rode in, finding narrow cobbled streets and ramshackle houses and sheds dominated by huge warehouses of the merchant lords. At length he found an inn. And he found also a girl.

vi. *The Perushka*

KADJI HAD rented a place in the stables of the inn for his pony and was striding the streets bound for the nearest bazaar when he saw her.

She was gloriously fair, slim and strong and no older than he, if as old. Her hair was a banner of dark red flame and her eyes, large and bold and startling in her clear tanned face, were smoky amber flaked with fiery gold. She had proud young breasts and a free-swinging stride that reminded him of the wild Kozanga girls; like them, she wore high boots and tight leggings which displayed the slim clean lines of her long legs.

It puzzled him as to what she might be. No daughter of the merchant lords or princely artisans of Nabdoor would walk alone in the streets, for the townsmen were fiercely protective of their women and kept them behind walls; when, as seldom chanced, they were permitted abroad in the two town streets, they went heavily veiled and in giggling groups guarded by eunuchs. Not so, the flamehaired girl with eyes of smoky gold. She walked as freely as if she had no master—and no father, either. He was baffled, intrigued, and also—attracted.

While he shopped at the booths of the bazaar, selecting dried meats and preserved fruits and black bread and an oiled sack of red wine for his long ride to the north, he eyed her. She might be, he guessed, a Perushka—a gypsy—for she wore the loose flapping *aftar* of that people, and the gaudy kerchief about her brows, and the gold bangles at earlobe and throat and wrist. But she did not have the roguish swagger, the bold flirtatious eye, the flaunting walk, which marked the Perushka women.

And there was one thing else.

By her side paced a gigantic plains-wolf, grey as smoke, with eyes of lambent golden fire. The bazaar-folk gave it and its mistress a wide berth, he noticed, and indeed it was a strange thing, and almost unheard of, for the wolf was as tame as a great dog. And yet it was purebred plains-wolf, untainted in blood with town-dog strain, for often had Kadji seen the terrible wolf-packs of the Great Plains, and had fought them betimes, when harsh winter made them fierce mankillers.

She was an enigma, and as he went to sleep that night in a cramped loft atop the inn, the mystery of the girl and the beauty of her filled his thoughts and floated in his dreams.

WHEN HE rose with dawn from his narrow pallet, it was to shiver in the cold raw breeze. The harsh bleak light of morning flooded the little loft and through the one small window, shielded with a carven *uthrab* screen of pierced wood, he could see the grey light on stucco domes and low-roofed houses, and a clouded wintry sky beyond to the World's Edge.

He broke his morning fast in the tavern of the inn, before a roaring scarlet fire, while a cheerful inn-girl with red cheeks and thick braids and a very dirty apron clattered pots and pans noisily. When he went to the stables to say good morning to Haral, his boots crunched on frozen mud crusted with a very light fall of snow. The cold season was upon the world, and henceforth the going would be hard and difficult.

The black pony was happy to see him, stamped restively and nudged him with its velvet nose while he gentled the steed with soft loving words and wove his fingers through its long unshorn mane. Today he must finish the last of his purchases and depart. He thought of the amber-eyed Perushka girl with her flaming hair: soon she would only be a fading memory to him, a bright-haired wraith. For once he left the streets of Nabdoor-town behind in his travels, he would never see her again.

He growled at himself, as a boy will: why all this accursed mooning over a pretty girl glimpsed in passing amid the streets of this nameless and unimportant little town? He was glooming over her like a love-struck poet, but he was no poet but a warrior, a man, and on a mighty mission of honor and vengeance! He had no time to dream about pretty girls; he should be meditating on blood and fire and steel. . . .

Yet somehow he could not drive her from his mind. And as he strode about the snowy streets, buying provisions for his pony, his thoughts returned again and again to the slim, proud, lovely girl with eyes of smoky amber and hair like a scarlet banner tossed on fiery winds, and on the great wolf that went ever at her side.

Almost he thought to see her again today, but no, she was nowhere to be seen, and Kadji did not care to ask too many questions of the boothkeepers in the bazaar. For here and there about the square strode burly knights of the Rashemba in their glittering longshirts of chain mail, horned helmets of sparkling steel on their straw-colored hair, their heavy red faces impassive, and cold grey eyes roving everywhere, alert and suspicious. To ask questions might mean to draw attention to himself; therefore Kadji asked no one about the flame-haired girl.

He kept his mouth shut and his face blankly incurious. He bought his goods with a minimum of talking, and he kept as far away from the towering horned knights as he could, without seeming to do so. And under his fringed *kuruz* the God-Axe, the Axe of Thom-Ra, lay bound against his beating heart. The sacred "Fortune" of the Chayyim Kozanga Nomads rode with him . . . and the razory edge of the holy steel thirsted to drink deep of the vile blood of the dog-knights of Rashemba.

vii. The Road North

ERE THE sun star Kylix had ascended to the zenith of noon, Kadji had finished purchasing his provisions. He settled his debt to the innkeeper, paid for stabling his pony, mounted and rode forth from Nabdoor. The sleepy Rashemba knights merely waved him through the gates without a word of query; still and all, the Red Hawk did not breathe freely until he had left the shadow of the walls of Nabdoor-town far behind.

Ahead of him, grim and bleak under the grey wintry sky, the endless plains of whispering grasses stretched north and ever north to the gates of golden Khôr and the fulfillment of his mighty Quest. He turned his pony onto the caravan road to Khôr and rode with a blithe heart and a merry song on his lips under the lowering sky.

The air was crisp and clear and cold, and the wind which sprang up with late afternoon had a sharp biting edge like a steel knife, but he pulled his fringed cloak more closely about him and rode on. It was a small joy to the youth to know that every hour brought him nearer to his goal; that with every league he rode he drew closer to the Dragon Throne, and to the dreamed-of confrontation with the shrinking and cowardly black-heart that sat in the sacred chair and wore the false name of Holy Yakthodah, and to the epic moment of glory when through his hands the Axe of Thom-Ra would strike down the Usurper on the high seat of his power, amidst the fat greedy *kugars* and the venal and cunning Rashemba knights.

What would happen after that proud and splendid moment, the boy Kadji could not envision. His dream stopped with the fall of Shamad the False . . . what would happen thereafter, Kadji could not guess. Doubtless he would die himself in the very next moment, cut down by the enraged knights of Prince Bayazin of Rashemba . . .

Perhaps. Very likely.

At any rate, he somehow did not see himself riding this same road south again, through the Barren Hills and the streets of Nabdoor, fording the level waters of the Babdar, and thence south across the Great Plains to the black mountains within whose hidden and secret heart his lordly grandfather Zarouk awaited his coming.

THE RED HAWK rode north as sunset filled the west with flame and rode on under bright stars as the first of the Seven Moons arose to fill the skies with silvern light.

He slept that night beside a flickering fire in the grasses and rose with first dawn to ride on. North and ever north.

And as he rode, Kadji the Red Hawk of the Chayyim Kozanga did not guess or dream that his feet were set upon the first leagues of a journey that would take him across the measureless face of the world to its legended and unknown very Edge, and to a strange and marvelous destiny before the gates of shining Ithombar the City of the Immortals.

Nor that his name would live in song ten thousand years.

Part Two

IN GOLDEN KHÔR

O life is short—and death is long—
'Tis joy to live, and joy to slay!
Out swords and life the battle-song:
A man can die but once, they say!
—*Road Song of the Kozanga Nomads*

i. The Coming of Kadji

IT WAS with dawn the Red Hawk rode proudly into high and golden Khôr.

Heaven was a canopy of golden silk shot through and through with flamy tints, and the lofty towers and tall spires of the imperial city caught and held the first shafts of brilliant day and blazed with a glory of flame.

Nor was it by mere accident or chance that Kadji chose the hour of dawn for his entry into the Dragon Emperor's city. He knew that guards who have watched the gates all night, marching their weary rounds upon the crest of the mighty wall, would at dawn be thinking more of breakfast and a soft warm couch than of catching an outlaw or piercing a disguise.

And also, at this hour, the gate road was flooded with early travelers: heralds in the imperial scarlet and silver, bearing scrolls sealed in hollow segments of the horns of unicorns; farmers with groaning wains, eager to be first at market; all manner of priests in black robes, sorcerers in purple, soothsayers in prophetic green, bound for the shrines, temples, holstelries and librariums of the great city.

In such a thick and motley throng, a lone warrior can easily lose himself; thus Kadji used a fat puffing old pedlar in soiled and tattered blue, mounted upon a fat waddling grey mare, to block himself from the view of the guardians of the gate, sleepy-eyed and brusk though they were.

He suffered the torments of the illicit, for a moment or two, when the fat old pedlar stopped dead before one of the guards and loudly asked the way to a good inn. The boy bent his head as if to adjust his leggings and fumbled with sweating fingers at the leathern thongs while the pedlar and the guard discussed the merits of this or that hostelry, and finally came to a mutual agreement on an establishment called the House of the Seven Moons.

But then the pedlar, bobbing his bald head in courtesy to the surly Rashemba knight, thumped his bare heels in the ribs of his mare and she went clopping forward, with the boy Kadji on his black Feridoon pony closely behind, and he was inside the frowning walls of golden Khôr.

Once he was past the scrutiny of the gate guards, Kadji turned his black pony into one of the broad avenues that radiated out like spokes from the hub of a wheel from the palace-crowned hill that lay at the heart of Khôr. All about him was hurry and bustle, even at this early hour: fat greasy *kugars* borne by tawny Easterling slaves in sumptuous palanquins, guardsmen on horseback and beggars afoot, court ladies in veiled conveyances, archers in clattering companies, merchants, laborers, priests. The broad avenues were thronged with hundreds of men and women, and amidst the crush and flurry, the Nomad boy felt lost and alone and out of place. He rode about aimlessly for a while, as the sun star Kylix climbed higher and ever higher in the azure dome of heaven; getting the feel and flavor of the Dragon City.

He cast a carefully casual glance or two at the high walls and gleaming towers and golden domes of the Khalidûr, the Citadel of the Dragon, as the imperial fortress-palace was called. To seek an audience with Shamad the Impostor openly was futile and foolish: he must come to stand before the Dragon Throne by some subterfuge, some subtle scheme. Doubtless one would occur to him—later. In the meanwhile he rode the city streets and gazed upon the myriad marvels of the world's greatest and most splendid capital.

Never—as it chanced—had the boy Kadji been within the walls of imperial Khôr. Even when he rode with his sword-brothers to establish the false Yakthodah on the holy throne, he had not entered the golden gates but had remained behind in the Nomad camp. Now was he here in truth—and alone!

Jubilation bubbled up in the boy's heart; but his head was cool, and he did not fail to see that it would be exceedingly difficult to make his entry into the fortress of Khalidûr. For whole companies of imperial scarlet-and-silver guards watched the gates—the Dragon Guard, they were called, he knew, and their number was made up of foreigners and Rashemba knights and mercenaries from distant and strange kingdoms.

About the base of the mountainous citadel, which was almost a small city in itself, and which the folk of Khôr called the "Inner City," ran a deep rushing moat as broad as a river. Guard towers stood at either end of the seven bridges that spanned this moat, and the heart of Kadji sank in gloom as he saw that every person who sought entry to the citadel was stripped and searched and disarmed of any weapon whatsoever, even to the smallest dagger.

Getting in would not be easy.

Getting out again might prove impossible.

However, he would worry about such problems later. *Suffice it for the moment the troubles thereof, and let tomorrow's trouble await the morrow*—or so ran the old saying of the Chayyim Kozanga Nomads.

He had at least gained entry into Khôr, and that without arousing the suspicions of any person.

And thus came Kadji to the Dragon City, and the first part of his Quest was accomplished.

ii. The House of the Seven Moons

HIS MORNING tour of Khôr finished, the boy turned off into a maze of side streets and began searching for a hostelry. The first such that he encountered bore painted on a shield hung above the courtyard gate the emblem of seven red crescents. This must be, he guessed, that same House of the Seven Moons whereof the fat pedlar had inquired of the gate guardians. On impulse he decided to stop here, as he was weary and hungry and cold.

The inns of Khôr, it seemed, were very different from the rude and rickety little inns, simple fare and rough housing he had sampled days earlier at the little hill town of Nabdoor. He could see the difference the moment he guided his pony through the portal emblazoned with the Sign of the Seven Moons.

Within he found a broad stone-paved courtyard, swept spotless, and a livery-clad stableboy to take the reins of his pony popped up on the instant, as if conjured into being by a magician.

The main hall of the hostelry was very large and low-ceilinged, stone walls and pillars washed in clean plaster of snowy white and warm peach and creamy rose. There was not just one but three mighty hearths with great fires roaring against the biting chill of the day, and scurrying scullery boys greasing and salting and spicing the mighty slabs of beef turning on slow creaking spits over the thundering fires.

The hall was crowded, despite the early hour, and men sprawled drinking at long low wooden tables. They were drinking vintage wine from rare glass bottles and stoppered earthenware pots, rather than sour beer or cheap ale from leathern jacks. These things the boy

40

noted at once, and not without certain qualms, for although his purse was well-stuffed with gold and silver
coin, it was not bottomless—Zarouk had seen him well-
furnished of pocket, reminded of the aphorism that the
man who pays his way liberally goes a smooth road,
while he who pinches his purse is ever in suspicion.

A fat, oily innkeeper with a smooth smile and cold
ugly eyes greeted him effusively and found a room for
him on the third floor of the establishment, though at a
price that caused the boy warrior to wince visibly.
These necessaries accomplished, and a livery-clad serv-
ingman having carried his saddlebags up to his room,
Kadji turned aside into the hall and found a place for
himself near the fire and ordered a hearty meal, although not without wondering how much it would cost
him. When he asked, with a forced and false casualness,
the serving girl named a figure so extreme that he had to
bite his lip against crying out the word "thievery!"—
and, sourly, the boy reflected that with prices like these
he would have to accomplish his Quest swiftly or find
himself sleeping empty-pocketed in some alleyway.

Kadji devoured the meal with relish, despite the cost,
and was finishing his pastry when the noise of an altercation forced itself upon his attention.

While eating, the boy had noticed in an offhand manner the arrival of a *kugar* lordling into the inn's main
hall, for the man made so much noise slamming in
through the door, and such a great affair of shaking off
the snow from his overcloak, and such a proud display
of ruffled sleeve and velvet sash and gold buttons that
he could hardly be ignored. For all that he was already
flushed and somewhat the worse for wine, the young
lordling loudly called for more, and so peremptory were
his several needs that it took three hurrying maids to
settle and serve him. Seated as if throned, booted feet
thrust out before him, the *kugar* rudely stared about

him at the others in so offensive a manner that Kadji wondered how the boorish fellow survived from day to day without getting into continuous fights.

He little dreamed that before the world was an hour older he would be facing this same *kugar* with naked steel himself.

IT WAS a sudden explosion of thunderous bellowings that drew Kadji's attention to the scene.

The *kugar* had been sprawled out, feet rudely thrust wide, blocking the aisle between the long low tables, and, it seemed, a passing fellow had stumbled over them. Instead of making his apologies for causing the other man to stumble, the *kugar* sprang to his feet with a roar of rage and hurled a string of epithets at the inoffensive fellow. Looking up, Kadji saw that the man was a little old man, lean and bony, in the grey robes of a wizard. A small, timid, inoffensive old man he seemed, with worried and watery eyes, slitted in the Easterling fashion, his yellowy head shaven but for a black queue, his hands buried in the capacious sleeves of his wizard robes, which, Kadji saw, were soiled and patched and tattered. This was odd, for the House of the Seven Moons catered most obviously to those whose purses were well-stuffed with gold coin. But there was no time to dwell on this peculiarity now, for events were exploding into a quarrel.

The mousey little wizard had been pattering down the narrow aisle between the crowded benches when his lean and bony shanks collided with the outstretched legs of the noisy, red-faced young lout of a *kugar*. The old man, his head bowed on his chest in deep thought or meditation, had not spied the spread-out legs of the drunken and offensive young lordling, and he had stumbled over them. Squealing in dismay, the wizard staggered, tripped, and nearly fell. Thrusting out his hands to steady himself, he had the bad luck to strike the *kugar's* arm just as the surly young lordling was hoisting a full goblet of fiery liquor to his lips. When he joggled the lordling's arm, the cup went flying, and so did the expensive purple beverage therein.

The *kugar* surged to his feet with an inarticulate roar of rage, and stood there with fire gleaming in his bloodshot, piggish, squinting little eyes, while the purple brandy dripped from his soaked japon and velvets.

Now, as, attracted by the disturbance, Kadji looked up, it was to see the poor old wizard shrinking beneath torrents of verbal abuse, fumbling for apologetic words, frightened gaze roaming about, while the burly young lordling, who towered over him with one red hand clenched on the hilt of his curved sabre, bellowed the vilest and coarsest insults at the old man from the top of his voice.

The little wizard was confused and bewildered and stammered for polite words; the *kugar*, younger by twenty years and taller by half a yard, glared down at him, red-faced and roaring, little pig-eyes fierce and brilliant and alive with the pleasure of a born bully.

"You foul-breathed, toad-hearted, stinking lump of dung! Dirty my boots, will you! Kick my feet out of your way, will you! Stinking gob of an Easterling whore! I'll wash my boot-leather in your filthy blood, you white-gutted old turd!" roared the red-faced young lordling.

"Highborn and most noble lord;" the timid little man protested, stammering in alarm and gazing about with frightened eyes as if to enlist the aid of the others in the hall, "I swear to the Gods I mean no harm! This lowly and most insignificant one intended no insult to your lordly self! Ten thousand apologies if this vile one has given offense! I beg you—I pray you—accept these humble apologies, and permit an old man to pass and take his weary bones to bed!"

His bleating tones were drowned beneath the bull-throated bellow of the *kugar*. And, as they wandered in pitiful pleading from face to face, meeting only indifference or derision, the frightened eyes of the little wizard came at last to rest on the face of Kadji.

"Pass, is it, you reeking lump of filth! To your bed, eh? Not likely, pig of an Easterling—more like, to your grave!"

And the *kugar* clapped his hand again on the hilt of his sabre and made to draw it from its scabbard of oiled leather. But he did not. For a hand seized his wrist and held it in a grip like iron. Kadji's hand.

iii. *The Honor of Cyrib Jashpode*

THE ROOM became silent as death, save for the sussuration of indrawn breath as many men sucked in their teeth, and the muted thump and clatter as men moved awyay to clear a space.

"You *touch* me . . . you dare to *lay hands* upon me!" The face of the young *kugar* lordling went pale with astonishment and he stared as if marveling into the grim serious eyes of Kadji.

Kadji spoke in low, quiet tones, and his words were courteous. "I pray you, lord, that you permit this poor old man to pass by without harm, and that you do the kindness to accept his apology for stumbling against your feet; and I beg your pardon for this interference, but, look, lord! The man is old enough to be your father, or mine: and he hath no steel. Surely the young noble lord would not draw steel on a harmless old man incapable of defending himself!"

The little pig-eyes stared marveling down at the boy

and in wondering tones the blond *kugar* repeated: "You lay hands on me . . . you dare to lay your dirty paws on the Highborn . . . you, a dog-gutted whelp of Ushamtar gutters? *Harool*"

And yelping a shrill cry the lordling whipped his hand loose from Kadji's grip and gave him a ringing slap across the face.

Kadji went white to the lips, for to strike another is the deadliest of all insults. And he knew that now he must fight. He stepped back and drew from beneath his garments the sacred Axe of Thom-Ra—for he bore no other weapon—and kissed it, making silent apology to the War Prince of the Gods that he must employ the God-Axe in so ignoble a cause as a wineshop brawl, and saluted the *kugar* with great courtesy.

"I am high Ioga of Yuzan, a Free Sword of the Ushamtar Nomads," he said in formal salutation, using the false identity he had assumed for the duration of this adventure.

The *kugar* laughed and spat and ripped off his velvets and the ruffled silk of his japon, revealing a bronzed and well-threwed torso. He unsheathed his sabre and kissed it to Kadji, growling out his own salutation in a slurred and careless fashion.

"I am the Highborn Cyrib Jashpode of the House of the Jashpodine," he grunted, and without further warning or ado swung a vicious back-handed slash at Kadji's throat. But, lithe as a dancing girl, the boy sprang backwards so that the blade whistled past him to go *thunk* in the wood of the table-edge, with such impact that Jashpode staggered and almost lost his footing.

The Red Hawk might have slain the *kugar* in that same moment, for the lordling could not at once disengage his blade from the heavy wood, but he did not, instead stood courteously to one side with the Axe lowered while the other with some effort wrenched his sword free of the grip of the wood.

Now wild with fury at the mild words and courteous manner of the Nomad youth, the young lordling sprang upon Kadji with a veritable whirlwind of blows. Steel rang against steel, filling the raftered hall with war's ringing music. Again and again, with effortless ease, the slim brown Kozanga lad turned aside the slashing strokes of the *kugar's* sabre. And ere long the heavier youth, somewhat the worse for drink and flabby in the muscles, became scarlet-faced with exertion and glistening with perspiration. He roared the vilest of insults at the silent boy, but before long he had to save his breath to fight with. And soon he was purple-faced and panting and staggering, his torso glittering and slick with sweat.

By contrast, Kadji was bone-dry, silent, and he breathed shallowly, showing no sign of exertion. Nor had he once taken a stroke with his great steel Axe, but restrained himself to merely warding off or turning aside the strokes of his opponent. This, though none but he knew it, was the silent vow he had made to his warrior Gods before entering the contest: that if he must employ the Sacred Axe in so lowly a combat, he would merely use it to defend himself, not to slay.

Around and around the long table they went, Jashpode panting gustily, dripping sweat; the Nomad youth as silent as a stalking panther. The boy had fought many hours with the axe and the sword, for the double-bladed war axe was one of the favorite weapons of the Kozanga Nomads; he knew that it had certain advantages against the sword—especially the sabre, which is slim and curved and can only be used to slash—and he was awaiting the proper moment to employ the weapon in a manner he knew. But it must be just the right moment.

It came: He caught the other's blade and twisted his

wrist, allowing the glistening curve of steel to slide up the axeblade to the hook at its peak; therein it caught firmly, and he twisted his wrist very suddenly the other way.

The narrow curving blade snapped in two pieces with a ringing clash that filled the hall. And Jashpode was disarmed.

Now, according to the code of the duel, as fought in the realms of the Dragon Emperor, it was well within the rights of Kadji to slay the other man. Instead he saluted politely and returned the Axe to its place beneath his fringed cloak, then turned away, taking the old wizard by the arm to escort him to his room, leaving the *kugar* behind, bare-handed, weaponless, weak with exhaustion and trembling with inarticulate fury.

All the way up the wooden stair the fat little wizard marveled at the prowess of Kadji the Red Hawk. And the youth answered the old man politely but modestly.

Thus it was that on the first day of entering the city of the Dragon Emperor, Kadji, Red Hawk of the Kozanga Nomads, made a friend.

And an enemy, too. For he had affronted the honor of Cyrib Jashpode, and that honor could be cleansed only in scarlet blood.

iv. Akthoob

THE NEXT day Kadji continued his tour of the magnificent city and even the desperate importance of his Quest did not deter him from admiring the splendor that lay about him to either side. For thirty centuries of time golden Khôr had ruled these lands, and in all those ages it had drunk deep of the rivers of gold that poured through the hands of its merchants and landowners. Emperor after emperor had added new jewels to its crown, until by this age it was a splendor of arch and forum, temple and theatre, colonnade and sepulchre. Broad, level avenues were lined with heroic statuary; memorials to triumphant and fabulous wars, the glories of long-dead monarchs and extinct dynasties.

At evening he made his way back to the House of the Seven Moons, but before he had even reached that quarter of the city he was fortunate enough to catch a glimpse of the man whose death was the goal of his Quest and the sacred duty laid upon him by the Lord Chieftain of the Chayyim Kozanga.

There was a crash of golden trumpets; heralds armed with ceremonial whips rode clattering through the street and the throng of citizens rapidly drew to the sides thereof, and among them was Kadji. A moment later a troop of mounted and gaily caparisoned nobles rode past, laughing and jesting, and amidst them all, one tall golden man shone. He was serene and beautiful, with a cold, sculptured face and ice-grey eyes, and when he laughed, as he did both often and loudly, Kadji saw that the laughter did not reach beyond his lips, for his eyes remained frozen and watchful and arrogant. Thus he was watched as Yakthodah the Holy Dragon Emperor rode past under a cloud of fluttering banners in the noontide of his glory.

As he passed, on his way to an evening of revelry at the theatre or the hippodrome, he turned by chance and his arrogant, icy gaze flickered over Kadji's face. For a single instant they stared into each other's eyes, the traitor and the avenger, before the Dragon rode on. And the keen eyes of Kadji noted that the cold beautiful face of the Emperor bore a strange small flaw. Directly below the corner of his mouth was a bright scarlet mark the shape of a *tarisk* leaf.

And then the Emperor was past the place where Kadji stood, and Kadji noted with widening eyes the curious and horrible creature who rode at the Emperor's back.

It was no man but a monster with the broad, sloping shoulders of a giant and the long, powerful, dangling arms and short, bowed legs of an ape. The thing went naked save for a harness of belted straps, and with amazement Kadji saw that its body was covered with glittering snake-scales, sapphire blue. It had a hideous broad hairless head, thrusting forward from bowed, enormous shoulders, neckless, noseless, scaled blue, with weird eyes of dull scarlet. In his astonishment, the boy uttered an ejaculation.

The man who stood next to him in the crowd chuckled at his cry of revulsion. " 'Tis naught to fear, young sir, for that is Zamog, the Holy Emperor's familiar, as we call him—one of the Dragonmen of the Swamp Country. They say he is as intelligent as an ordinary man and utterly devoted to his master."

Kadji turned to murmur polite thanks to the man beside him and recognized him for the small, timid Easterling wizard he had saved from the bullying of Cyrib Jashpode the evening before.

The wizard nodded and grinned: "Aye, young sir, I knew you at a glance, and could not help speaking, for still this lowly and insignificant one owes you a debt of gratitude for your gallant and chivalrous deed! I am Akthoob of Zool, a minor practitioner of the Art Sorcerous and Magical, drawn hither to perform my small and unimpressive craft before the Holy Emperor, whom, or so this person has been told, delights in exhibitions of magic, and has a liberal hand with gold for those fortunate enough to entertain him! But, come, if you are on your way back to our mutual hostelry, let us walk together, and perchance you will permit this person to join you at supper, so that we may converse further and at our leisure. . . ."

KADJI FOUND the garrulous old wizard amusing and informative company. Over a fine dinner of jellied eels and spicy herb broth that evening he drew the fellow out. Akthoob, as was his name, had never been in golden Khôr ere this, but knew it well from converse with other magicians in his coventicle. Like all of his Easterling race, Akthoob was loose of tongue and thus it was not difficult to guide the conversation in the directions Kadji desired. Passing himself off as one Ioga of Yuzan, a Free Sword or mercenary-for-hire, come from the territories of the Ushamtar Nomads, Kadji expressed the curiosity concerning the city and its emperor proper in an outlander but new-come to the mighty capitol.

Akthoob, he learned, had already applied to the Chamberlain for permission to enter the sealed gates of the Khalidûr and perform magic before the Imperial court. His pass was dated two nights hence.

Their meal done, and Kadji yawning with sleepiness, they parted—effusively wishing the young warrior a good rest, old Akthoob went to his chamber and Kadji to his own. But not to sleep. The Easterling wizard had described the hundreds of alert and wary archers and swordsmen who guarded every portal of the Khalidûr, and Kadji lay awake far into morning, his brain bewildered, examining first this plan and then the next. When finally he dropped into an uneasy and fitful slumber, it was on a hopeless note.

There seemed to be no way he could enter the palace and strike down the Impostor.

v. *The Flamehaired Girl*

THE NEXT day dawned with dim ruddy light filtering through a fall of snow. The air was crisp and biting cold, and Haral stamped and neighed, its breath a plume of vapor on the frosty air as Kadji led the black pony from its stall.

Hooves crunching on crusted snow, they rode the circuit of the city that day while the Red Hawk continued his explorations. This day he had set aside for studying the gates of the city, their number and positioning, the approaches thereto, and the manner in which they were under guard.

Returning toward sunfall when Kylix was a disc of red gold sinking behind the towers of the western quarter of Khôr, the Nomad boy made a strange discovery.

As he guided his pony into the long Avenue of the Hippogriffs that led to the House of the Seven Moons, a young woman was borne past him in a princely palanquin veiled in gauzy silks and carried by strong slaves in gold-and-purple livery.

The inquisitive youth had studied the nobility of Khôr. He knew that the *kugars*, the greedy class of great landowners, used no livery, being wealthy but not armigerous. The Emperor permitted a blank white escutcheon to the *kugar* class as a whole, but only the old Imperial baronial families had the distinction of color liveries. And gold-and-purple, he knew, were the colors borne by an ancient family close to the dynasty currently regnant: a royal house, however, considered extinct.

Thus his attention was drawn to this closely veiled palanquin through curiosity, and by this chance he was

51

able to observe something he might easily otherwise have missed.

Just as they drew together, side by side in the stream of traffic, the slaves bearing the palanquin slipped in an area of slick, icy wet snow, and staggered for a moment. This caused the flap of the veils wherewith the sides of the palanquin were draped to fall back, revealing the features of the personage who rode within.

For a single flashing instant of time Kadji found himself gazing straight into smoky eyes of amberous gold, huge dark-lashed eyes set in a clear tanned oval face framed in a gorgeous mane of flamy-golden hair.

It was the girl he had seen in Nabdoor, to the very life!

His eyes widened in surprise, and he caught, in that flashing instant before the flap fell back, a similar expression of surprise on the girl's face. She had recognized him, as well.

He reined up his black Feridoon pony and watched the palanquin go by in bafflement. The girl he had seen in Nabdoor had gone unattended save by a monstrous grey plains-wolf. And she had been dressed in ragged and voluminous garments like a wandering Perushka wench. But this girl rode like a princess, and her slim young body was sheathed in expensive silk, and pearls, the great blond pearls of Nizamar, had been woven like a net through her glorious tresses, and a great green opal had glowed at her brow.

Surely the two girls were one and the same—or *were* they?

On sudden impulse, he guided Haral aside to follow in the wake of the veiled palanquin. It turned in to a courtyard much overgrown and where the ruins of a garden grown wild lay dead and black and tangled beneath the deathly fall of the filtering snow.

The mansion that rose in tiered height beyond the

walled courtyard was splendid and ornate, virtually a palace. But it was festooned with dead vines and the carven stonework at balcony and architrave was weather-stained. Such dilapidated grandeur in decay could have been caused only by long years of neglect . . . as if the mansion had stood empty and unattended for some space of time.

At the corner of the street whereon rose the mansion, Kadji found a small wineshop; he tethered his shivering pony to the wooden bar at the door and went in and ordered a tankard of ale, mindful of his shrinking purse.

Those who frequented the wineshop were, he saw, grooms and squires, gardeners and servants employed hereabouts, and thus a reservoir of gossip. He unlocked their tongues by buying a drink for all, for the moment pretending to be a genial mercenary swordsman on a drinking spree. Before long he learned that the mansion was the House of the Turmalin, that it had in truth stood deserted for many years, since, in fact, the death of the last Emperor, Azakour, some twenty years before. The Lady of the Turmalin had fled the city during the struggles of dynastic succession, and had taken up her abode in a far province.

"But surely the noble maiden I glimpsed going in just now is too young to have deserted Khôr twenty years ago!" Kadji said.

One of the grooms winked and nodded.

"Aye, this be her daughter, the Lady Thyra, new come from the provinces," he said.

And that was all Kadji could discover. He rode back to the House of the Seven Moons through the blowing snow, deep in thought. Was the girl of the palanquin the same girl he had seen as a ragged Perushka in the traders' town far to the south? They were alike as sisters, nay, more so: Kadji was convinced they were one and the same

But why this should bother him, he could not discern. What was it to him that a strange and beautiful girl had been in Nabdoor some days ago, and now was here in mighty Khôr?

The snow was thicker now. Great parties of *kugars* were moving through the slushy streets in the direction of their quarter, which ringed the central Khalidûr like a half-moon. All day he had seen the *kugars* gathering into the capital and had thought but little of it, save to keep a wary eye out for the Highborn Cyrib Jashpode, the young *kugar* lordling whom he had angered and fought, and with whom he guessed there would yet be a final reckoning.

He dined alone that evening while the snow storm rose and raged beyond the shuttered windows. The friendly Easterling wizard, Akthoob, was not in evidence this night. And as the bony and talkative little old man was the closest thing to a friend he had yet made in this vast, bewildering, many-peopled metropolis, the Nomad boy felt oddly lonely as he ate his meal alone.

There was shouting in the streets and many horsemen rode by and the sound of blown bugles somewhat later, but the boy Kadji, nursing a frugal jack of ale with a full belly beside the warm hearth, paid no attention. Then, toward the first hour after midnight, the inn door came crashing open with a blast of icy air and a flurry of swirling snowflakes, and the Easterling, Akthoob, came in, white from head to foot with snow, his pointed nose blue with cold, his slitted eyes watering, blowing on his frozen hands and stamping the caked snow from his fur-covered buskins.

Kadji hailed him. "Come, friend, share the fire and a jack of ale, for the night is cold and ark."

Suppressed excitement glittered in the slant black eyes within that long, sallow face.

54

"Colder and darker than you think, young sir," replied the little wizard in tense low tones.

"What do you mean?"

"The *kugars* have arisen. Holy Yakthodah lies dead in the Khalidûr, cut down by a *kugar* knife. And a *kugar* council rules golden Khôr this night!"

vi. The Death of the Dragon

ERE DAWN the word had sped to every corner of Khôr and not a miserable beggar shivering in his hovel but knew that the last legitimate heir of the dynasty was slain, that the great House of Azakour was extinguished at last, and a grim and bloody time of troubles had come upon the Dragon Empire. The savage and merciless struggle for power would begin now, and there were many men of Khôr who could well recall the terrible days that followed the death of Azakour Third twenty years agone, and how all of the Plains had been torn asunder by civil war until the discovery of a legitimate heir—even that same Yakthodah who lay now in state in the Throne Hall.

The facts behind these bloody and swift-moving events were easy to unravel. The *kugars* had seized power after the death of the Emperor Azakour, and only an army of Rashemba knights, lent to the Pretender, Yakthodah, by his supporter and father-in-law, the High Prince Bayazin, had driven the greedy *kugars* from the place of power. The Nomad warriors of the Great Plains had aided in that war, but no sooner had they assisted in establishing Yakthodah in his father's holy throne, than the fickle Emperor, discovering he needed the friendship and the fat purses of the *kugars* to sustain him in the life of revelry and license he desired, had welcomed back with open arms the rich and power-

55

ful landowner class. From this point things had gone from bad to worse, even to the point of alienating, then outlawing, and finally making war against the stout and loyal-hearted Nomads.

But the *kugars* were not completely satisfied. They feared the influence of Bayazin, and the strong hold he had on the pleasure-loving Yakthodah. And recent news that Bayazin, with an army of his mighty Rashemba knights, was now moving upon Khôr—ostensibly to pay a visit of state upon his royal son-in-law, and also to garrison the heartlands about Khôr against the long-expected revenge of the Kozanga Nomads—drove the jealous and fearful *kugars* into open rebellion. Yakthodah had been assassinated by night in his own Throne Hall, and *kugar* mercenaries now held the Khalidûr fortress, and the gates of Khôr itself against the expected siege of Prince Bayazin.

In all the turmoil and chaos that made the very world echo to the collapse of dynasties and the battle of opposed regimes, what of the boy Kadji, Red Hawk of the Chayyim Kozanga Nomads, and his sacred Quest to avenge upon the body of the man the world believed to be the True Emperor the stained honor of the Kozanga war clans?

What indeed? It would seem that a *kugar* blade had spared him the task his grandfather had set upon his shoulders.

He made up his mind swiftly, for time was very important: by noon, it might be, Khôr would be in a state of siege. If he were to act at all, he must do so *now*.

"Akthoob, have you still that pass which permits you entry into the Khalidûr?"

The old wizard shrugged bony shoulders. "This humble person has it here in his purse, young sir, but what good? I shall not now use it, as the Holy Dragon Emperor before whom I would have performed my small arts lies now stark and cold as last morning's bacon. . . ."

"Does the pass describe the purpose of your visit?" Kadji pressed urgently through the fog of words.

"No, no indeed: it merely says that one Akthoob of Zool is given permission to enter into the Khalidûr and to come into the Throne Hall . . ."

"And it is dated?"

"Aye, young sir, but why all these questions? Oh, very well! It bears tomorrow's date, as I told you when we talked . . ."

"You mean, *today's* date, surely! For dawn is not many hours away, and the folk of Khôr reckon a day as beginning one hour past midnight, do they not?" urged Kadji.

"Very well, then, today's date, surely, but why do you ask all of these questions . . ."

Grim purpose burned in the boy's clear bright eyes, and determination could be seen in the firm set of his jaw.

"You are in my debt, are you not, Akthoob, for that I saved you a beating from the hands of that *kugar* bully, Jashpode, and mayhap saved your life, indeed?"

"Yes, yes, to be sure, young sir, but I do not—"

"I like it not, that I must force you to endanger yourself, old man, but my cause is very urgent, and as I see it we shall not be any great hazard, if all goes well. But now I fear I must ask you to absolve yourself of your debt to me, by doing me a favor . . ."

"A favor? *What* favor, young sir?" Curiosity glittered in the slant black eyes.

In short words Kadji answered him and watched the curiosity turn first to consternation, then astonishment, and finally—to terror.

vii. The Double Impostor

SURPRISINGLY ENOUGH, it proved no great task to enter the Khalidûr. True, the bridges that spanned the moat, and the gates and portals through which they must passed, were under very heavy guard, and those guards were not the burly, red-faced Rashemba knights (most of whom, Kadji learned, had been brutally massacred during the first swift, crimson hours following the assasination of the Emperor, and those survivors now disarmed, under guard, or fled) but nervous, truculent *kugar* hirelings.

The odd thing was that one glance at their pass sufficed to win them past guardpost after guardpost, and generally without any questioning at all. Kadji, garbed for this expedition in sober robes and betraying no signs of either his true Kozanga identity or his assumed Ushamtar guise, had frankly expected keen questioning to expose the falsity of their purpose. And while he did not expect arrest, he would not have been surprised had the guards at the very first checkpoint brusquely turned them back, refusing to let them pass.

In preparation for this he had bidden the old wizard to clothe himself in most unwizardly raiment: sober and nondescript, but expensive garments in good taste.

As it was, their pass,—after all a valid one,—saw them through the hazardous moments of scrutiny and ere long they stood within the vaulted halls of the Khalidûr, and both of them could begin to breathe again.

The explanation of the miraculous ease whereby they had passed the sentinels of the Khalidûr was simple. A dynasty had fallen in the first hours of dawn; and now, in the earliest hours of morning, a new regime was being put together. Hundreds of people were streaming in and out of the royal fortress, important *kugar* lords bound for council meetings, young lordlings, boys, messengers and the like, scurrying back and forth with screeds and notes, commands and memoranda. No individual with a proper pass could safely be stopped for questioning, for no guard could be certain—in this uneasy and disquiet time—whom he could offend with impunity. The most insignificant-looking fellow might by tomorrow wield terrifying powers of life and death over the remnants of an empire. Hence they passed through swiftly.

The immense pile of the ancient Khalidûr was murmurous with sound, whispering conversations in the corners, the footsteps of hurrying pages and message-bearers, the bustle of important lords. In the busy throng no one bothered even to notice the presence of two unfamiliar faces, here where so very much was new and where so many faces were those of strangers.

Hardly caring to risk stopping a passerby to ask him the way, Kadji and old Akthoob found their way through the shadowy and labyrinthine ways of the vast fortress by a combination of lucky accident and inspired guesswork. Without wasting too much of their time, they gained the entrance of the great Throne Hall at last.

For the rest of his life Kadji never forgot that moment. And yet, oddly enough, he could hardly remember the hall itself, one of the wonders of the world, with its soaring columns like a forest of stone trees, its stupendous dome, its glistening and mirrorlike pave of slick black marble. From the moment they stumbled upon their goal his attention was riveted on the thing that lay under a scarlet-and-gold cloth at the foot of the throne itself.

The throne—as for it, he spared hardly a glance at the glorious and immeasurably ancient seat of imperial power. True, it was fashioned entirely of pure and solid gold, and contained in itself the ransom of a province; true, the hand of some long-dead genius had lavished a lifetime of skill in the fashioning of it, for it was formed into the likeness of a coiled and glittering dragon whose arched wings rose enormous, and whose uplifted head was a snarling and terrible fanged mask of ferocity with eyes that glistened like orbs of flame. Two gigantical fire-rubies were those eyes, and their like the remainder of all this world could not afford. But Kadji saw it not, the Dragon Throne, for his eyes were fixed upon that which lay at its foot, on the lowest of the nine tiers of the dais whereupon the throne stood.

A young woman was bending over the covered body as the two entered the hall, and Kadji seized his companion's arm and shoved the old Easterling wizard into the shadow of a column from which they could watch unobserved.

The woman drew back the torn tapestry a little as if to reassure herself that it was truly the dead Emperor who lay there. For a long moment she looked, ignored by the guards who stood about the throne with stolid and indifferent faces. Then she drew up the cloth again and turned away to make her way swiftly and purposefully out of the hall.

As she glided away her path took her directly into the glare of gold light from massed candles, and Kadji sucked in his breath with amazement and wonder. For it was—*Thyra!* The mystery girl he had glimpsed many days ago, disguised as a wandering Perushka lass, in the little village of Nabdoor—the girl he had seen but recently borne through the streets of kingly Khôr like a princess!

What was the secret of the flamehaired girl who so often crossed his path? The boy's tanned face settled grimly: he must face one mystery at a time. And so he but watched helplessly as the strange young woman left the Throne Hall and vanished from his view.

Then, with the nervous wizard at his heels, Kadji rapidly crossed the length of the hall and approached the throne and that which lay at its foot. The body was sprawled on the lowest step of the dais, and a rich tapestry had been hastily torn down to cover the dead thing. Kadji stepped nearer, despite Akthoob's fearful admonitions; he shrugged off the restraining hand the little Easterling laid on his arm. He must make certain that this was in truth the body of the man all the world thought to be Yakthodah but he knew as Shamad the Impostor. He bent over it but he could not see its face because of the torn tapestry. Greatly daring, he reached out and drew aside one corner of the covering, exposing the head and breast of the corpse.

Akthoob turned pale as milk and gestured feebly, but Kadji ignored him and bent closer, straining to see in the dim wavering light of distant candles.

There were *kugar* mercenaries stationed about the throne to guard the body, but they gazed stolidly ahead and paid Kadji no attention. It was naught to them who came to gaze upon or mock or revile the body of the Holy Emperor. In the general uncertainty of the times, they, like the sentinels at the gate, did not care to earn the enmity of any strange or unfamiliar person who might, ere long, turn out a man of power with a long memory.

So Kadji turned back the blood-stained tapestry and gazed without hindrance upon the face beneath.

It was cold and white as marble in death, and death had robbed it of much of its beautiful perfection. The mouth was drawn in a frozen grimace of terror or outrage or surprise (who could say?) and the glazed, unseeing eyes stared up forever at the unknown face of the assassin.

Many knives had done the fearful deed—or perchance but one knife, striking many times. For the corpse bore frightful wounds in breast and shoulder, belly, throat, and side. It lay in a pool of drying blood, sticky and glutinous and vile.

Only one wound was visible on the face of Yakthodah, and that was in the cheek. Part of the lower face was slashed and gory, and Kadji noted without saying anything that the wound had obliterated that portion of the face that had borne the scarlet leaf-shaped birthmark he had noticed yesterday when he had watched this man riding through the streets on his way to a night of revelry—

"Come; look," he bade Akthoob.

The old wizard shuddered and rolled up his eyes but did not dare make too vocal a protest with the guards so near. He shuffled timorously over to where the Red Hawk stood and peered down with frightened eyes at the gory horror beneath the cloth.

"Is that Yakthodah?" the boy asked in a low whisper.

"Of course—who else should it be?"

"But *is* it? Look closely; you saw him yesterday as clearly as did I."

Akthoob shuddered and turned away.

"Whoever he was yesterday, he is dead meat today . . . let us be gone from this accursed palace, young sir, I beg of you."

"In a moment. Look again . . . look at his jaws," he said.

"What of it? The Holy Emperor did not have time to shave before they . . . they . . . cannot we go now, while we yet have whole skins? What if the man be not shaved?"

"Nothing, perchance," frowned Kadji. "But . . . somehow it seems odd that his beard-stubble should be so long. Yestereve, when we saw him riding by, the Emperor was cleanly shaven . . . but this is no one night's crop of whiskers . . . it looks like this man had not shaved in two days, perchance three: . . . Had the Emperor anyone in his court who resembled him?"

"Haii, gods, will you stand here talking when any moment we might be . . . well, and how should I know?" whimpered the wizard fretfully.

"Think," Kadji insisted. "You were in the Khalidûr at least once ere now, were you not, to be interviewed by the Chancellor so that you might obtain permission to perform before the court. Saw you anyone who resembled the Emperor?"

"Well . . . yes, now that you remind me of it, this humble person did indeed notice a minor functionary . . . a handsome youth with an extreme pallor and light eyes . . . he did look somewhat like the Holy Dragon Emperor. I remember thinking so at the time, although it had quite passed out of my mind . . ."

Kadji replaced the tapestry and turned away, striding thoughtfully across the hall. The guards regarded him with stolid indifference. At one of the exits from the hall, he exclaimed suddenly, and turned, excitement lighting up his face.

"What is it now?" groaned the Easterling.

"Where is Zamog?" Kadji demanded fiercely.

"Wha . . . the Dragonman? Why . . ."

"Yes! The loyal monsterling that went ever at his master's back; surely, to have struck down the Emperor, the assassin would first have had to slay the faithful Zamog."

A strange light dawned in Akthoob's slitted eyes.

"Can it be . . . ?"

"Yakthodah was slain right there, where his body now lies; and the body of Zamog the Dragonman should be hereabouts, if he is dead. But where is it? Nowhere! And why should they have bothered to carry away the corpse of the blue-scaled one? Kick it into a corner and forget it, let it lie—*that's* how they would have thought, under the pressure of swift events! If Zamog is not here, it means the monsterling is not slain; and if Zamog is not slain . . ."

Excitement flared in the face of Akthoob.

"What is this you are saying! Does this humble one understand you to suggest . . ."

"Yes. That is not the body of Yakthodah, but of another. The man you knew as Yakthodah is an impostor named Shamad. He yet lives; he has fled—doubtless, fled the city itself."

Kadji laughed, a boyish, reckless laugh, dangerous in this shadowy and murmurous place filled with eyes and ears. He cocked an irreverent thumb back at the hacked corpse.

"That dead man is a double impostor . . . *and Shamad lives!*"

Part Three

TWO RODE EAST

The world is wide—the seas are deep—
  A man must go a warrior's way!
Let the women wail and weep:
  A man can die but once, they say!
                —*Road Song of the Kozanga Nomads*

i. Questions and Answers

THE SNOW had stopped and they rode back toward the House of the Seven Moons under a clear sky of hard wintry blue. And as they left the towering cliff of the Khalidôr behind, little Akthoob visibly relaxed and gradually became his talkative old self again. He plied Kadji with questions, and as for the Red Hawk, he answered them truthfully enough, for he felt he owed the old wizard that much courtesy at least.

"*Aii*, then you are not a Free Sword of the Ushamtar, as this lowly one had been given to believe, but an assassin of the Kozanga Nomads, dispatched by your lordly chieftain to slay the false Emperor! This humble person begins to understand . . ."

"To understand what, old man?"

Akthoob shrugged, but there was a hint of laughter in his slanted black eyes.

"The manner in which you fought with the young lord of the *kugars*," he explained. "This elderly one has seen the Ushamtar warriors in battle, and also, once, the noble-hearted heroes of the Chayyim Kozanga. And your mode and method of fighting, young sir, were purely Kozanga and in no wise similar to the Ushamtar . . ."

Kadji winced a little at how swiftly and easily an observant eye had penetrated his imposture. "Let us hope the Highborn Cyrib Jashpode is not so observant as you, old man; for now that the *kugar* lords are in control of the city, it would not do for me to have aroused the slightest suspicions in the mind of one who already has a grudge against me!"

"Ay, 'twould not do, this one agrees," the old wizard shuddered. Then, changing the subject: "But tell me, young Kadji (if this humble person may call you that by that name), what has become of the living Shamad? Think you that he has concealed himself in some corner or cranny of imperial Khôr? Surely he could not have fled the city—not with the *kugars*, his deadly enemies, in control of all gates?"

Kadji frowned thoughtfully and chewed his lower lip.

"Shamad must have been warned, of the impending plot and substituted his hapless look-alike for himself; I would not put it past him to have forced the young functionary who so closely resembled himself to put on the imperial regalia—and then murder the unfortunate youth with his own hand, leaving the corpse for the *kugars* to see when they came to slay him. In the confusion, the *kugars* might well suppose others of their plot had already done the deed . . . but as to whether Shamad still dwells within the walls of Khôr or not, who can say? If he gambles on the swift arrival of his ally, Bayazin the High Prince, then he might well be hidden somewhere in the warren of the Khalidûr, awaiting the Rashemba host to seize the city . . . but methinks not. Shamad cannot know how long the *kugar* force can hold the city against Rashemba siege: I believe he has fled the city; he and his monstrous Dragonman servant; for, should the High Prince break the *kugars*, the impostor can always return in triumph from hiding."

"*Aii*, but how could he get out, with his dearest enemies holding every gate and entryway?"

Kadji smiled grimly.

"The sword-brothers of my clan have a saying, old man—'Gold is a key can open any gate'—and Shamad must have amassed much of the beautiful metal during his brief regime! And not all of the gates of Khôr are huge and heavy-guarded . . . yesterday as I studied the gates, I noted a small, obscure, seldom-used postern gate in the eastern wall of the city; Shamad and his pet monster could have gained it with ease, through the labyrinth of alleyways in the eastern quarter. It gives out on the empty plain, to be sure, but Shamad could have ridden east a ways and then turned aside to take the Grand Chemedis Road, the mighty highway across the plains the merchant caravans use. I wonder if it could be thus. . . ."

The little wizard shyly cleared his throat. "*Ahem!* Perhaps this small and insignificant person can assist you," he suggested diffidently.

"In what manner?"

"This lowly one has some poor learning in the Art Sorcerous . . . to be precise, young sir, this person knows an art by which the minds of one or two men can be made blinded, fascinated, enrapt, and thereupon can be made to divulge any information they may possess . . ."

Kadji frowned. "Does it work? We don't want to arouse any suspicions . . ."

Akthoob smiled affably. "Leave it to this person—but come, we near our hostelry . . . what is toward?"

Kadji had seen it, too, and reined his black Feridoon pony to a standstill. For a host of *kugar* swordsmen invested the courtyard of their inn, and among them he glimpsed the face of Cyrib Jashpode.

ii. The Mind Jewel

IN HASTY confusion, they turned their steeds aside into a narrow, cobbled alley and rode its length, emerging into the Street of Monoliths, which led in the opposite direction from the boulevard on which was the House of the Seven Moons.

The little wizard was moaning with fear, and Kadji himself was tense and distressed. He could not be certain, but it looked as if the young *kugar* bully, now doubtless in a position of some influence, since his class had seized control of the regime, had returned in strength to have his revenge on Kadji for the humiliation he had received at the hands of the young Kozanga warrior.

At any rate, Kadji did not intend to ride into the jaws of the wolf in order to ascertain his mood. Forewarned was forearmed, as the saying had it. He would take refuge elsewhere, but there was no reason the old Easterling wizard should any longer be involved in his troubles, and it might well prove dangerous to the old man should he be. So he suggested they part company here.

Akthoob was not happy at the thought. He pointed out that the anger of Cyrib Jashpode might well be aimed at himself as well as Kadji, since his clumsiness had been the cause of the trouble. The Nomad youth could see the sense of the argument. They debated as to a possible course of action.

Since Shamad had perhaps already fled from Khôr, according to Kadji's theory, the boy no longer had any reason to linger in the troubled city. And to remain in Khôr might be to involve him in the civil war and the coming siege: he was anxious to be gone and on the road in pursuit of his wily and cunning quarry. Akthoob, too, had no wish to endure the miseries of the siege or the vengeance of the *kugar* bully, and would prefer to leave the dust of Khôr behind him. So they resolved to ride without further delay directly to the little unused postern gate whereof Kadji had spoken; if possible, they might discover that Shamad had, in truth, left the city by that means; at worst, they could leave the city themselves by that ill-guarded way. Under the lowering sky of afternoon they crossed the city by means of alleys and side-streets and drew up before the postern where two sleepy *kugar* mercenaries, wrapped in fleece-lined cloaks, huddled about a small iron cauldron of smouldering coals.

"Permit this lowly person to do the talking," Akthoob hissed, and Kadji nodded and remained in the saddle while the little Easterling dismounted and walked over to the guards, plucking something from a pocket of his robes, perhaps a coin to bribe their passage.

Kadji watched with narrow, alert eyes as the little old man ambled over to the surly guards, nodding and bowing in his timid, self-effacing way, while all the time a flow of courteous speech poured from his lips. The thing he had drawn from the concealed pocket was a gem, a luminous and twinkling crystal, and as he babbled on, the wizard turned the crystal between his fingers in an absentminded way, as if through nervous habit.

To the guards, the jewel was a potential bribe, and one of princely value, and they eyed it with greedy interest, not noticing that as Akthoob turned it and played with it, the gem became alive with glittering lights that played in a bewildering and mesmerizing fashion over their faces. Amber and coral and rose, azure and palest yellow and opal blue, the twinkling lights of the sorcerous gem played across their stolid, unshaven, loutish features. And all the while their greedy little pig-eyes followed the shimmering lights of the moving gem while Akthoob talked on and on in a low murmurous voice.

At length the moving play of colored lights held them bedazzled. It was as if their minds were asleep while their bodies remained awake. One even let go of his heavy spear which fell to the frost-crusted cobbles with a clang and a clatter that Kadji thought was enough to wake the dead—but the two guards did not even seem to hear the noise. They listened sleepily to the low sing-song voice of the little wizard and, after a time, began to answer his interrogations in dull grunting tones, too low for the young warrior to hear.

Finally Akthoob turned away from them, opening the postern gate and then returning to his mare. The flashing jewel he carefully stowed away in his voluminous garments.

"It worked, I gather?" Kadji grinned.

Akthoob nodded in bland satisfaction. "The mind jewel seldom fails. Yonder *kugars* tell that just before dawn two men bribed their way through this same gate with much gold—"

"Two men? Did they describe them?"

"Unfortunately, they could not see their features, for they were robed and cowled in black garments like priests. But one of the men was hulking and brutish, like a great ape, and the other, who conducted the bribery, had smooth white hands, strong and fair and well-kept, like a princely lord. The guards say the two rode east in considerable haste."

"Then I am right! I must be right—it could be none other than Shamad and Zamog, his reptilian slave!"

The old Easterling shrugged. "Doubtless the young sir was correct in his assumptions. However, the guards also state that one other person used this gate, and that but recently, scarce an hour ago."

"Could they describe him, at least?"

"Alas, it was not a *him;* it was a young woman," replied Akthoob.

Kadji gasped, and swore feelingly.

"A young girl—my own age—a flamehaired girl with smoky amber eyes?"

"I cannot say. She, too, went heavily robed against the cold wind; my two friends yonder could not describe her appearance, save that her saddle was silver-mounted, and her robes of expensive fur."

It is that girl again—Thyra—the girl we glimpsed

looking at the corpse at the foot of the throne—it *must* be her!" Kadji growled. "At every twist and turn of the way, I encounter this girl! She is a puzzle, aye, a great puzzle . . ."

"They say she rode alone, but that there was a great dog with her, like a tame wolf," offered the little wizard.

Kadji grinned. "Aye, the grey plains-wolf, her pet. Then it *is* the girl Thyra! But why should she have left the city? Could she be in pursuit of Shamad as well as we?"

"I know not the answer to these riddles, young Kadji, but if this lowly person may suggest haste . . . yon two guards remain 'mazed and bewildered by the art of the mind crystal, and I have opened the gates for our passage. We should be on our way, for the power of the jewel will not hold them in the magic slumber for very much longer."

And so Kadji, accompanied by the little Easterling wizard, rode forth from imperial Khôr on a bleak wintry late afternoon, and turned east on the tracks of Shamad the Impostor.

The boy thought that with luck they might catch up to the fleeing traitor ere nightfall, for the Impostor could have no suspicions that he was being followed.

Kadji was determined to ride as far as was needful, however.

He did not dream how far his journey would take him in truth. Had he somehow known, he might well have turned back. As it was he rode on into the gathering shadows, following the triple trail of tracks across the snowy ground . . . east and ever east they led, and the Red Hawk and the little wizard followed ever after.

iii. Flaming Eyes

WHEN IT became too dark to any longer follow the trail, Kadji was forced to halt, to make camp amidst the frozen plains, and to wait for day.

Because they had so swiftly left the city to avoid the vengeance of the *kugar* Jashpode, they had with them neither those of their belongings which had been left behind in the inn nor any provisions whatever. But Akthoob had cleverly "borrowed" the winesack wherewith the two guards of the postern gate had been driving off the chill, together with a few wheaten cakes one of the guards had been munching. So it was not entirely on empty bellies that the two travelers went to sleep that night, wrapped in their saddleblankets and curled about a small fire.

WHEN THEY woke to the first light of dawn, Kadji cursed with great feeling. For soft fat flakes of white snow were falling and, from the thick white blanket that covered the ground, had obviously been falling for an hour or two. Thus the slight track left by Shamad in his flight was now hopelessly obscured.

Refreshing themselves with the last of the wine and some crumbs of the wheaten cakes that were left, the two mounted and rode on due east through a driving blizzard that steadily grew worse until at length Kadji could no longer perceive their direction from the position of the sunstar Kylix, as the sky was one blowing mass of freezing whiteness. He dared go on no further, lest in the blind flurry of snow they deviate from the eastward and wander aside, thus losing whatever small advantage they had, for by now he reckoned they were not far behind Shamad, who could have had no reason to have pressed his flight with such tenacity and vigor as had the vengeful Red Hawk of the Kozanga Nomads.

They had halted on a low rise of ground and Kadji was debating whether it would not be wise to try to pin their blankets together into a crude tent, and thus wait out the storm in relative comfort, when his black Feridoon pony lifted its head alertly, sniffing the freezing air, and gave voice to a harsh neigh of danger.

In a moment, Kadji, too, had heard the distant sounds that had aroused his pony to a sense of peril.

Wolves!

The eerie chorus of their distant howling came faintly to his ears, as if the blanket of snow muffled their hunting cry. But he knew the sound for what it was: Somewhere out there on the snowy plains, a pack of gigantic wolves were circling their helpless quarry, narrowing in for the kill.

It was a vagrant wisp of thought that made him ground out a bitter curse and seize up the reins, pulling his pony about and heading his nose into the wind. His booted feet thumped the pony's ribs, and without a word of explanation to his companion, the boy warrior was off and had vanished into the flurry of snow. Like an avenging demon the Red Hawk hurtled through the whiteness, praying to his grim Nomad Gods that he not be late . . . for it had occurred to him that the quarry the hunting wolves sought might well be his enemy, Shamad! And it was before the sacred Axe of Thom-Ra that the cunning and traitorous Impostor must fall, not to the glistening fangs and hungry jaws of a pack of plains-wolves. . . .

Within moments he saw them. Their grey hides made them all but invisible in the snowy murk, but their eyes of flaming green were visible, like a host of goblin moons, burning weirdly through the snow-streaked gloom.

He burst among them like a thunderbolt, and the great Axe was in his hands, flying through the air in terrible whistling curves like a live thing, shearing its irresistible way through the thick fur at throat and flank, hacking a gory way through tough muscle and heavy flesh of shoulder and neck.

The wolves broke into a vengeful howling chorus at the sudden appearance of this new and unexpected adversary. One sprang snarling for his face, but the heavy Axe caught it in mid-leap and flung it back to the snowy earth, maimed and broken. A second wolf leaped upon him and clung for a second, claws buried in saddle-leather, foaming jaws snapping at his breast, lambent eyes of emerald flame burning like mad moons into his own. The Axe came whistling down and clove its head to a flying splatter of crimson and broken bone, and it fell and was lost behind.

Then he was through the circling wolves and rode up to where their quarry sat astride a great grey mare, muffled in furry robes. There was no time for words—no time for anything but fighting, for the wolves were upon them now and Kadji was very busy for the next few minutes, wielding the flying Axe. But he did not fight alone: the fur-clad one was fighting, too, with a flashing rapier that drifted as lightly as a ray of light, drinking deep of wolf-gore as it ripped like a steely needle through throat and side. Haral fought, too. The brave little pony was shod with steel, and as the steed reared back on its hind legs, it churned the air with forehooves that struck like meteors amid the mass of ravening wolves. More than one went down to death with the hoofmark of the black Feridoon pony stamped deep in broken skull and splattered brains.

In a moment or two more it was over, for the wolves

had lost heavily, and turned from their quarry to tear asunder their own fallen, to snarl and snap and quarrel over their own dead.

And then a weird shape loomed out of the murk and came flying toward them, and it was Akthoob. The little Easterling wizard was pale and chattering with terror as he rode through the wolfpack, but he was fighting nonetheless, in his own way, with flashes of violet flame that spurted from his trembling fingertips with an audible crack, like a whip, though muffled and dulled by the blanketing snow. In a moment he was through the raging wolves and reined up with a palsied hand beside the boy warrior.

The plains-wolves were in the retreat now, dragging their dead away to be devoured at leisure and in safety from these strange beings who fought and slew so terribly, not only with cutting steel, which they knew all about, but with miniature bolts of purplish lightning, which were frightening and wholly new to their experience.

One wolf there was that did not flee; indeed, he seemed to be fighting on their side, and came trotting back after the others had been driven away. And Kadji thought he knew that grey phantom with burning gold eyes, and turned to its master with a thrilling surmise, to see who it was he had rescued from the ravening fangs. And found himself staring into the white, tense, but beautiful face of a young slim girl with eyes of smoky and amberous gold, under a flying banner of flame-red hair.

iv. Thyra

HE MUST have called her name aloud in his surprise, for she turned curious eyes upon him.

"You seem to know my name, warrior," she said in a clear voice like a pure golden bell. "But I know you not . . . unless . . . yes! I *have* seen you before; in Nabdoor, was it not, although you were dressed differently then—"

"So were you!" he returned, and she laughed, a lovely sound.

"So I was, come to think of it! But then you went robed in an Ushamtar *kuruz,* with leggings, and girdle, and belled cap . . . whereas now you look more like one of the Kozanga clansmen than any Ushamtar . . ."

Kadji grinned; upon quitting Khôr he had thrown off the Ushamtar garments and donned his true tribal raiment, which fortunately he had concealed in Haral's saddlebags against discovery.

"I am Kadji the Red Hawk, the son of Goraky the Tall, who was the son of Zarouk the Lord Chief of the Chayyim Kozanga Nomads," he said proudly. "And I have seen you—*you* three times: once in Nabdoor, when you went in ragged scarlet like a wench of the Perushka; the second time in the streets of Khôr, when you went in the fine silks of an Imperial princess; and the third time in the great halls of the Khalidûr, when you looked upon the naked face of him men believe to be Yakthodah the Holy Dragon Emperor . . . but whom both you and I know to be a vile and villainous impostor!"

Her eyes widened in incredulous amazement, and he laughed in a gush of loud, boyish humor at her expression. But she did not contradict him—it was obvious that she was following the flight of Shamad, too, for she had looked on the face of the dead man and must have known, even as had Kadji and Akthoob, that he was not the True Emperor.

Before she could speak, the little Easterling, whining and snuffling, spoke up miserably.

"The snow falls heavier and yet more heavy, and we sit here talking as if 'twere the balmy breezes of spring caressing our frozen ears, and not winter's bitter blasts," he complained. "Can we not bundle our saddle-blankets together into some fashion of tent, to shield us against the blizzard?"

"There is no need," Thyra offered quickly "I have a small tent stored on my mare, and collapsible tent-poles. If we all work together, perchance we can put it up, even in this heavy snow . . . and then we can rest and talk in comfort."

THE TENT was not easily erected in the rising gale, cumbered with the weight of thick-falling snow; but at length, and with much exertion, it was erected, and proved surprisingly capacious, although once three horses, three people, and an enormous grey wolf had entered and the tent flap was sealed against the wind, it was somewhat crowded.

Thyra's plans seemed to have been made far in advance, as if she had received some premonition of Shamad's flight and the rising of the *kugars*. For the wicker-work pannier her mare had borne disgorged other supplies besides the tent: food and drink, and even a shallow porcelain dish of charcoal, which Akthoob set aflame with a solemn magical Word and a mystic sign of his left hand. As the baking warmth of the ruddy charcoal steamed his garments dry and thawed out his numb and icy exterior, Kadji relaxed, pillowed comfortably on his own saddle and blanket-roll, stretching out his feet toward the cherry glow of the coals, and reflected that there were worse companions to take along on a journey than a magician. Such personages came in handy at times.

And so they ate and drank, frugally, and fed meal to the cold and weary horses, and all the while the mighty smoke-grey wolf sat by his mistress and regarded them with unblinking eyes of gold fire. The wolf made Akthoob uneasy and he kept moving his own saddle and blanket-roll closer to Kadji.

"You need not fear Bazan, little man," Thyra smiled. "He is a friend to those I name my friends, and only a foe to my foes."

"Aii," whimpered the timid little wizard, eyeing the great wolf uncomfortably. "Then this person humbles himself, and begs that you will make doubly certain he understand Akthoob to be his very great friend, indeed. Perhaps then the lord wolf will cease regarding this lowly one as though he were a dumpling!"

Thyra and Kadji laughed at the notion that anyone could mistake the lean and scrawny little Easterling for a plump and edible morsel.

Ere long the heat of the fire and the warmth of the wine made them drowsy, and Kadji doubly so, for that he had enjoyed no sleep the night before, and by now it was certainly early evening, although one could not be certain as the sky was a blind mass of falling snow.

They slept that night in cozy if cramped quarters, while beyond the tent the demons of the storm howled and the Seven Moons hid their shining visages behind veils of flying snow.

v. A Princess of the Blood

IT WAS past dawn when the woke, and the snowfall had ceased at last, and all the world was a shimmering plain of utter white under a fierce but impotent sun.

They breakfasted frugally from Thyra's store, washed themselves in snow melted over the last embers of the coals, struck the tent and rode forth over immaculate fields.

Kadji was grim and worried. Yesterday they had been close on the heels of Shamad: now they had lost him, for surely the tracks of his passage were hidden beneath the snowy mantle. All they could do was to ride forward in the same direction, due east, hoping that he was continuing in the same direction. If, after a time, they did not come upon fresh tracks, they would know he had changed direction, perhaps riding south to strike the Grand Chemedis Road.

As they rode, Kadji and the girl saddle to saddle, the old wizard behind, nodding sleepily and dozing from time to time, the two young people talked in low tones. Kadji had told Thyra his story, and was curious to learn her own. When she did not elucidate the mystery of her presence in these events of her own accord, the boy warrior made so bold as to ask for it.

"You know my mission, and why I must pursue the Impostor at peril of my own life, so as to wreak the vengeance of my people upon him, and thus eradicate the stain laid upon the honor of my brethren. Shall I not know your own reasons and your story as well?"

"That is so," the girl said. "And if we are to be road companions, we should share our knowledge as we share our food. Ask, therefore, what you will."

"Who are you, really?"

81

"I am the Lady Thyra of the Turmalin House. My mother was Amazya the younger sister of the late Emperor, Azakour, Third of that Name. She died in a distant province when I was but a child, having fled the Dragon City on the death of her brother."

That was something to think on! Kadji was astounded and stared at her in silence for a bit.

"An Imperial princess, then," he said. The girl nodded, her flame-red hair rippling gloriously in the sunlight.

"But are you not the True Heir to the Dragon Throne?" he demanded in astonishment. "If you are the last surviving member of the dynasty, why . . . why . . ."

She shook her head firmly. "The Law states that a female shall not inherit, thus I have no claim upon the throne of my Uncle. But my false cousin, the so-called Yakthodah—"

"—Shamad of Perushk," Kadji murmured.

"Even so, although I did not know his true name," she continued: "The charlatan, Shamad, when he came to power, feared that the family of Azakour might perchance know him for a false Yakthodah, or might seek to dethrone him so that another of the Holy Blood could ascend the Dragon's Chair. Thus he pursued with his vengeance even to our distant province, to the west, and would have exterminated the last of our House. Alas, there were few to oppose him: my mother dead, my father long since in his tomb, and I but a child. But friends of my House had hid me away, disguised as a serving girl, so that the assassins could not find me, and bore back to the false Emperor word that the House of Turmalin was extinct to the last leaf of the last withered branch.

"I determined to seek out this false-hearted and murderous charlatan, and if he were not the True Emperor as my friends whispered, to expose him: for I knew certain things about the true appearance of the original and genuine Yakthodah that perchance he could not know, nor could any, since they were buried in family documents in the archives of the dynasty. I traveled in the guise of a Perushka girl, and as such you glimpsed me in the streets of Nabdoor; this I did because there were none would wonder to see a girl traveling alone, if she were in Perushka dress."

"Was it not unsafe for you to travel by yourself, a mere girl?" he asked.

She laughed again; she had the loveliest laugh the boy had ever heard. "Not with Bazan going ever at my side! For there be few bandits or thieves so foolhardy as to pick a fight with a full-grown wolf of the plains!"

"Why did you abandon your disguise in Khôr, and appear as your true self? Did not that place you in danger from Shamad?"

"Ah, but not in the least! For what could be done in distant Zoromesh—the province wherein I was reared —and openly, by assassins, can hardly be performed in the Imperial capital against an avowed Princess of the Blood. There are too many eyes to see, too many tongues to whisper, too many agile and cunning minds to speculate. I came into Khôr in state and presented irrefutable and documentary evidence of my lineage to the collegium of the heralds. Poor Shamad—I shall have to get used to that name!—was forced to publicly acknowledge me his royal cousin. I was extremely careful, you may be sure, that my palace was guarded against intrusion; and doubly certain never to leave myself alone with Shamad or any of his people. In public places, he could not easily contrive my assassination, and in private I took every precaution that it should be no less difficult. His only recourse was to—politely—ignore my existence as much as was possible, and keep as far from me as he could. I never let him learn that I suspected him for an impostor, although I soon enough determined that he was one. Ere I had maneuvered circumstances to a pass where I could expose him and ruin him, the intriguing *kugars* intervened with their stupid plots and the coup was accomplished. As a Princess of the Blood I could come and go freely in the Khalidûr at any time; thus it was not difficult for me to obtain a close view of Shamad. Even as did you, I recognized that the man on the steps of the dais was not Shamad but another. My people queried and bribed the gate guards and eventually discovered that Shamad and his Dragonman in disguise had fled the city on the very night of his pretended assassination; I made haste to follow."

"Why?" asked Kadji bluntly. "He is believed dead, and can no longer trouble you. The *kugars* have nothing against you, since a woman cannot inherit the Empire. Why not leave him alone?"

"You forget that he sought to slay me. *Me,* a Blood Princess, of the House of Holy Azakour! I, too, seek vengeance, even as you."

She bridled a little under his frank, quizzical gaze, and her small, determined chin lifted proudly.

"Oh, you need not look at me in that wise, young man! What have I to fear from the Impostor and his servant? I can use sword, lance and bow as well as any man—and Bazan, here, is a powerful ally! I could have slain both of them, I know it!"

He wisely held his tongue. There are times when it is not good to provoke a woman, and this was one of those times.

BY MIDDAY they had seen no trace of tracks on the snowy plains, and thus decided to veer south so as to join the Grand Chemedis Road. This broad highway spanned the plains from the remote satrapies of the Easterlings, to the Rashemba kingdoms of the west. If Shamad was bound east, they should encounter each other on the highway sooner or later; if he had doubled back, hoping to join forces with the High Prince Bayazin, then they had lost him for good.

By nightfall they reached the stone-paved way that led east and ever east across the world. They slept that night under a sky of black velvet, blazing with the fretted fire of a million stars.

For several days thereafter they continued following the stone highway east, until Khôr, its plots and dynasties, its sieges and thrones, dwindled far behind them. On the fifth day of their departure from the little postern gate in the wall of the Dragon City they came upon an encampment of Perushka.

vi. A Knife in the Dark

THE GYPSY caravan was drawn up in a semicircle beside the old highway, and a huge bonfire blazed in its center, as much to warm the wandering Perushka against the chill of winter nights as to keep away the plains-wolves who went famished in this bleak season and were often goaded by their near-starvation to attack men, even large parties.

Kadji was doubtful as to the wisdom of stopping to interrogate the chief of the Perushka caravan, for among his people they were despised as rogues, thieves, liars and vagabonds. But Thyra made mock of his hesitancy; she knew them well, and had learned their barbarous tongue as a child. Besides, she argued, even if the caravan had caught no glimpse of the two fugitives in their flight, they would doubtless permit Kadji to purchase food from them for red gold, and Thyra's store of provisions was almost exhausted since she had not planned on being forced to feed two extra mouths, to say nothing of the horses.

At length the boy let himself be shamed into following her plan, and they rode forward into the Perushka camp. The wagons were dilapidated and shabby, and the canvas that covered them was threadbare and patched in a thousand places. The Perushka themselves were a villainous-looking lot, with swarthy faces, filthy clothing and vicious eyes. Their women were bold and painted hussies, but the heavy application of cosmetics could not disguise knife-scars and the signs of disease. Even the dogs that came pouring out in a yelping chorus from under the wagons to herald the arrival of strangers were a mangy and mongrel lot, although they lost courage at the sight of mighty Bazan. As for the great grey wolf, he paced like a gliding, flame-eyed shadow at the heels of his mistress and ignored the hound-pack with the innate dignity of his kind.

The chief of the caravan was a lean, sallow, one-eyed rogue with a gap-toothed leer instead of a smile and a ragged fringe of whiskers that made him resemble one of the Hairy Men of the Hills of legend. Gold bangles flashed in his ears; bracelets jangled about his dirty wrists; a gaudy kerchief bound his scabby and unwashed scalp; and the thick reek of cheap perfume which clung to him did not even disguise the stench of his unwashed body or wine-stained clothes.

Akthoob, like most Easterlings, was a merchant at heart, which is to say that among his people the ancient craft of haggling over a price had long since risen to the level of one of the fine arts. Thus Kadji left it to the small wizard to conduct negotiations for the purchase of supplies. And as Thyra was the only one who had any familiarity with the Perushka tongue, he left it to her to question the chief as to whether he or his people had seen anything of the fleeing Shamad. This left him with nothing to do, so he stayed with the horses. He might be wrong about the Perushka being thieves and vagabonds, but there was no question but that they were past masters of the art of horse-stealing, and there was no one else to stand guard.

Kylix the sun star had long since sunk in crimson glory behind the western horizon of the world when his two companions returned from their separate missions.

Akthoob was beaming, his lank and bony face glowing with a smirk of self-satisfaction. By this, Kadji correctly guessed that the little wizard had purchased provisions for many days from the gypsies, and at a price not too exorbitant.

Thyra, too, was radiant with suppressed excitement.

"The chief—his name is Rukuz—says they saw two travelers at sunup, riding dead east along the highway. One was a tall, bright-haired man with white skin, but the other was lumpish and thick-set, and muffled in heavy robes. It can be no other than Shamad and Zamog!"

"Then they are, at most, only a day's journey ahead of us," Kadji said. "If we ride all night—pray to Mother Chaya there be no more snow—we could catch up to them by dawn."

"I think so . . . but, Kadji . . . old Rukuz has offered us the hospitality of his people tonight . . . they have boar roasting in the fires, and there will be singing and dancing . . ."

He gave her a strange look.

"Well, we cannot spare the time. And if that one-eyed old rogue is as villainous a blackguard as he looks, I would not trust his wine to be without a sleeping-potion mixed therein . . . or saw you not the twinkle in his eye when I gave Akthoob the purse of gold wherewith to buy provisions? I have seen naked cupidity in my

87

time, but the glint in his eye at the sound of the chink of gold coins was virtual lust. I wouldn't trust that old wolf any further than his own scruffy whiskers!"

The girl proved obstinate.

" 'Twould be an insult to refuse the hospitality of the caravan," said Thyra stiffly. "We would be doing Rukuz an affront to his dignity; and I know these people, Kadji. They may look a bit rough-avised, but they are good folk at heat. We *must* stay, if only for the meal . . ."

The youth set his jaw grimly. "I am one day behind the false Shamad, and I will not fall further behind him by a single hour. To the Nine Hells with Rukuz and his dignity! I am sworn to a sacred mission of vengeance and honor and I will ride to the World's Edge, if need be to strike down the traitorous Shamad! You may stay here for the 'singing and dancing' if you like; if these be such 'good folks at heart' as you claim, then you are safe in their company. But I am for the road."

There was fire in the girl's eyes but he paid it no heed. While she spluttered and argued he turned stiffly away and mounted his black Feridoon pony. Some of the Peruskha were drifting near to watch this altercation between the foreigners. Poor old Akthoob was flustered and apologetic, trying to calm the angry girl and appease the stiff-faced youth.

"Will you stay with her, old man, or do you ride with me?" Kadji demanded. He did not like the way the Perushka were gathering close about them. "Speak up! You owe me nothing, so if you wish to follow later with her and the wolf, I bid you farewell . . ."

"This lowly one is of the opinion, young sir, that— *aii!* Treachery!"

Kadji never learned the opinion which the skinny old Easterling wizard was about to give voice to, for in the next instant he felt heavy hands upon him and he was

88

dragged headlong from the back of the rearing squealing pony. It would seem that old Rukuz saw that fat, jingling purse of gold about to leave camp and ride away across the Great Plains, and had decided to enforce his hospitality upon them. Kadji was in no mood for such tricks. He swung about, half out of the saddle, and drove his bootheel full in the teeth of one swarthy, grinning Perushka rogue. Teeth snapped and crunched and the man fell away shrieking and spitting broken teeth and blood.

Then firelight flashed on polished steel and Kadji felt a blow strike him in the back. It was not a heavy blow: odd how numbness spread through his shoulders and arms. Strange how the world swung and swooped dizzily about him and the noise of the scuffle faded as if in vast dumb distances. He reached a curiously heavy hand to his back and drew it away red with blood.

Then he heard Akthoob yell and Thyra scream and the world went black and he fell forward and did not even feel it when he hit the ground....

vii. Flashing Swords!

HE MUST have been unconscious for only a few seconds, and he never knew what had roused him, unless perhaps it was the pain. Never had he felt such pain in all his young years ... red, raw, ripping pain that tore through him with every breath and brought him, gasping and tingling, awake.

He lay face-down in the muddy, trampled snow and his back and left shoulder were on fire, or so it felt. Dashing, dipping, swerving figures cavorted between him and the roaring bonfire at the center of the camp, and he watched them fuzzily for a few moments, wondering at their odd, ungainly dance. Then he saw it was fighting, and he heard a wolf growl and snap and a man scream, high and shrill like a woman. In the next instant he heard Thyra cry out some words in a desperate voice, and he came lurching to his feet, helping himself up by clutching to Haral's legs and bridle, for his pony stood very near as if to shield his fallen master from attack.

Akthoob and Thyra stood back to back in a circle of snarling Perushka rogues. The girl had a sword and was fighting superbly, steel rapier flickering in the firelight: even as he looked she gutted one bewhiskered rogue neatly, and parried the swing of a cutlass with a clang of steel on steel.

Akthoob was fighting off the attackers in the same way he had battled his way through the wolves—with flashing streaks of brilliant violet flame that flickered from his outstretched fingers. The timorous little old wizard might be pale and chattering with terror, but he fought like an avenging demon when need was at hand. As Kadji rubbed his eyes to clear his fuzzy vision he saw one Perushka villain stagger screaming from Akthoob wrapped in crackling flames.

But Bazan was the true hero of the battle. The great wolf ranged among the Perushka like a flame-eyed monster from the Nine Hells. His savage jaws crunched on bone and ripped through manflesh, spurting blood in showers on the trampled snow. With each ringing snap of his ferocious jaws a man died, his face torn away, his arm savaged, his guts spilling from a slashed stomach. The grey wolf killed and killed again.

Kadji dragged out the sacred Axe from beneath his garments and lurched and staggered into the mass of rogues. The pain had faded again; the numbness was back; but it was not enough to drag him swooning down as before, for his friends were in danger and he must fight. If he must die, at least let it be on his feet, in the teeth of the foe; then could he die happily, as a Chay-yim warrior should.

From somewhere within him the boy found the strength to lift the heavy Axe and begin that slow, re-morseless, and resistless sweep from side to side. So had the Kozanga axemen fought from the dawn of time, and it transformed one man into a terrible killing machine. He staggered into the massed Perushka, whose backs were to him, and the great swinging scythe of the Axe had felled five men before the Perushka even realized he yet lived.

Akthoob cried out in amazement to see Kadji on his feet and fighting, and Thyra looked with astonishment all over her white face; she had thought him slain.

He did not walk very well, so he took his stand, spread his feet wide, braced himself against the pull of the heavy Axe, and swung the glittering steel in the faces of the Perushka who turned their steel against him now. They perhaps did not know that cutlass, dirk or wicker shield cannot stand against the terrible swinging stroke of a Kozang axe. But they learned it soon enough. Swords snapped and dirks shattered against the whirling weight of that mighty blade. Shields were smashed to flying bits and the men that bore them were knocked from their feet with broken arms or dislocated shoulders or crushed ribs when they sought to ward off the great curving blows of the Axe of Thom-Ra. Men died about Kadji like flies.

The Blacksmith of Heaven had smelted and purified and tempered the steel of that immortal Axe, and it was from no worldly ore at all. The burnt-out core of a wandering and fallen star had given up that precious and unearthly metal. The War Prince of Gods had given that glorious and sacred weapon into the hands of the founder of Kadji's race, Kozang of Chaya. The divine blood of that ancient hero flowed yet in Kadji's veins, and as Kadji fought, in a red haze, fighting against the black shadows that thickened about his vision and strove to pull him down into the long sleep from which there is no awakening in this world, he chanted aloud the ringing staves of the age-old epic of his warrior people.

They would have been proud of him in this hour.

Now the Perushka had melted from before him like frost before the dawn of spring, and he must turn about for they were at his back. They crowded behind him, yapping and yelping and snarling like curs, when such strive to pull down a kingly stag. His feet were clumsy, for he could no longer feel his legs, but somehow or other he managed to turn about without interrupting the slow, sweeping rhythm of that terrible scarlet Axe. It was just as well, for had the rhythm faltered, the exhausted boy could never have found the strength to lift that mighty weight again. He was all but dead on his feet and he did not even know it.

And so he turned about to face them, and now the fire was at his back and he could see the cowardly fear written across their snarling faces, and the mirror flash of naked steel in their hands. Again and again the terrible scythe of that great steel Axe tore through them and its passage through their bodies did not even slow the tempo of the swinging strokes.

The Axe sang now, a weird hum and thrum, as it swung like a hideous pendulum through the bitterly cold air. The deep-throated song of its swing was loud in Kadji's ears, for he could hear nothing else now save the song of the Axe and the thunder of his heart beating, heavy and slow, and deep so that his whole body shook to the rhythm like the slow pulse of a mighty drum.

Now he could not even see, for blackness was before him and between him and the men he fought and slew so terribly. Black, black, all was black. And—*cold*. The coldness came seeping up through his body from the earth itself, as if he stood knee-deep in glacial ice. His legs he could no longer feel, and his arms were like two sticks of wood. His face was black with effort, his lungs were on fire, his teeth were bared in a fighting grin as terrible as a skull's, and yet he fought on.

And then he took the sword in his side. It came in low and under the ribs and it sank deep within him. He did not feel it, but he could feel the warm wetness spreading over his belly and down his thighs, as if a floodgate had been opened. And as the blood went out of him, his strength went too, as if the wound had loosed both at one blow. The Axe of Thom-Ra flew from his nerveless hands—striking yet another Perushka in the face, shattering his skull, and taking down to death yet one more foe, although he knew it not. And he fell forward and moved no more.

It had been a good fight, he thought. His grandfather would have approved.

And then there was nothing but the darkness.

Part Four

THE DARK TIME

And what if death be dark and near,
   And we be toys wherewith Gods play?
Though night be cold and filled with fear,
   A man can die but once, they say!
                —*Road Song of the Kozanga Nomads*

i. The Dreams

THE DARKNESS was deep and numb and thick, and
in it there were no sounds or sights or feelings. Not even
memories could penetrate the numb black womb which
cradled him. It was like what a tree must feel in the
blind and tongueless silence, in the deep slow half-sleep
of vegetable existence.

After a time there were visions, or dreams, but they
were confused and scattered and meant nothing to him.
There were faces that bent over him through a red blur,
the white face of a girl with frightened eyes, and an old
man's face, long-jawed and knobby and remarkably un-
handsome, with yellow skin and sad, slant black eyes.

And voices, too, dim whispers, like the echoes of far
converse. It seemed that people were arguing, something about whether or not to move him or to let him
lie. The girl was saying that they must get him under
shelter or he would freeze to death on the cold ground;
the little old man said that he was nine-tenths dead as it
was, for the point of the sword had nipped the lungs,
and with every breath he was drowning in his own
blood, and that to move him even a little would be to
kill him on the spot; no, no, they would have to drag a
tent over him, and leave him lying where he was . . .
and then the voices faded away and although he could
blurrily see the lips moving he could hear nothing, nothing at all.

THEN, A LONG while later, after he had spent a measureless eternity of frozen cold, there was warmth, slow
golden warmth, baking deep into the chill that bound
him. He basked in it thankfully, feeling the cold seep

out of his body drop by drop and he drowsily let his eyelids flutter and fall open and he could see warm red firelight dancing against the roof of a tent and painting huge monstrous black moving shadows. And there was someone by him, someone near, and he looked up at a long grey-furred muzzle, a wet black nose, and an open mouth with white fangs a-glisten and a long pink tongue.

The grey-furred face looked down at him with mute, questioning eyes, and sniffed at his face, and then the rasping pink tongue licked his face and he laughed a little, weakly . . . but that started the coughing again, the slow horrible racking coughing that he had lived with so long and had forgotten between sleeps, and a dirty, thin-faced girl with unkempt red hair came quickly to shoo away the dog—or was it a wolf?—and to hold the wet cloth at his nostrils so that he breathed again the good, clean, astringent spicy smell that seemed to dull the red pain in his lungs and to sooth the slow, racking fit of coughs. . . .

THEY WERE very strange, the dreams, each one different from the one he remembered before, and somehow he could not seem to summon the wits to piece them together into a fabric of meaning. It was like one of those painted puzzles sawn in many small segments that children piece together in play: but he could not seem to fit the pieces together. They remained bright, meaningless scraps.

There was another dream, filled with pain. He could not breathe; it was as if a hill was mounded upon his chest, and the pain of it, the heavy crushing weight, the close, stifling warmth, forced him to struggle up from the black sleep into the light again. And there was a girl bending over him, the same girl from before, he

98

thought, although much thinner, with great dark hollows beneath the eyes, and a thin, pinched, colorless mouth. She held a bright thing in her hands, cradled it, like a glowing coal. And behind her was the thin sallow-faced little man, mere skin and bones he was now, and there was fear written on his face. He was saying that it could not be done—whatever it was—and the girl, grim and tight around the mouth, kept repeating that it could and that it must, for he was drowning in his own blood . . . she kept muttering that strange phrase over and over again, like a curse, or a prayer.

The old man was trying to stop her, to seize her wrists, but she turned a fierce bright intolerable gaze on him that made him shrink away into a huddle.

"I am guilty," the girl said in a hard voice. "If he dies, I have killed him. For I was stupid and wrong and stubborn, and he was right—we should have left the camp at once, not lingered arguing until that black rogue of a Perushka dog struck him treacherously from behind with a knife."

And then she bent over him and did the thing she meant to do, and he felt a pain beyond all of the other intervals of pain, bright, blinding, incredible . . . and the blackness came again, and the deep sleep, and there were no dreams for a long time thereafter.

HE FELT like a drowning man must: the sleep that engulfed him was like a black, lightless sea, from which he emerged at intervals into the dim light of day, to gulp a breath or two of air before sinking below the suffocating waves again.

Once again he came swimming slowly up out of the black sea of sleep into the daylight, they were arguing.

"This person must remind the young woman that she has not slept in two days. She cannot long continue in

this manner, or old Akthoob will have two invalids on
his hands. . . ."

"I am fine; this is the crisis; if he comes through this
night safely, then he may yet mend . . . but it takes great
concentration . . . I must guide his sleeping body to re-
pair itself, for flesh can heal, and bone can mend, but
the lung . . ."

The girl, he saw fuzzily, was kneeling beside him, her
face blank and dead, her gaze turned inwardly. A small
spiral of green smoke crept from a pot clasped between
her knees and as she breathed in this spicy smoke it
seemed to him that her spirit departed from its house of
flesh and left only—vacancy.

Over her thin shoulder he saw the long bony face of
the old man. Slitted black eyes were narrowed thoughtfully, and his mouth was pursed as in distaste.

The old man said, in a low muttering voice: "Zoromesh . . . Zoromesh . . . it must be that . . . but why did
the girl *lie* to us?"

None of this made any sense to him, so he let go and
sank effortlessly once again down into the black sea of
sleep whose smothering waves rose hungrily about him
to suck him down to silence and restful ease. . . .

And after this there were no more dreams at all.

ii. Zoromesh

HE OPENED his eyes and gazed incuriously upon
strangeness.

There was a rough rocky roof above him, and stalac-
tites dangled therefrom like pendent spears of stone.

Curled up against his side, the great grey wolf slept,
its nose buried in its tail, like a huge friendly dog.
Bazan, that was the brute's name, he remembered.

He lay quite comfortably on folded blankets, and

saddlebags were heaped behind him, and he felt warm and cozy. A great lassitude enveloped him. There was no urgency in anything, no importance, and no hurry. He did not even feel curious, although nothing of what he saw around him did he at once understand.

Somewhere behind him, further back in the cave, a horse blew out its breath and stamped restlessly. He remembered that he had owned a horse once, a black Feridoon pony, but he could not recall its name or what had become of it.

The air about him was pleasantly cool and fresh, although it did savor somewhat of unwashed wolf, horse, and man-sweat. A fire was crackling off to his left, and he turned his head to look at it. Someone with patient labor had scooped out a hollow place in the hard-packed, rocky, earthen floor of the cave, lined it carefully with smooth flat stones, and a small neat fire of spicy wood and dry leaves crackled merrily thereupon. The blue smoke that rose from the flames smelled deliciously of pungent herbs.

A bracket of tough black wood was built above the flames, and a thick earthenware pot was suspended just above the fire. Within it some fluid seethed and bubbled. It was a good sound; a pleasant, homey sound. He remembered his mother's cookfire, that time the sword-brethren had wintered in the black mountains of Maroosh, where the Kozanga clans held a permanent settlement for the womenfolk and the younger children. Her hearth had been like this: warm, clean-swept, good-smelling.

Then a girl, bent over, came through the low opening of the cave, which was covered by a hanging fur. She came into the cave, glanced at him, saw that his eyes were open but made no comment, bent over the fire and examined the contents of the earthen pot.

She was thin and gaunt, as if she had not eaten well

in some time, and there were dark hollows and circles under her eyes as if she had gone long without sleep. Her thin body was muffled in heavy glossy furs, but the crudely made jacket was open, so it was not very cold outside. Beneath the furs she wore a threadbare man's tunic, much too large for her, and very patched.

Using her fur mittens for pot-holders she took the earthen container from its hook above the fire and brought it over to where he lay. She muttered a curt word, and the grey wolf stirred, got up, and slunk out of the cave, nosing its way through the flap of the fur covering that shielded the entrance. Then the thin, worn girl knelt at his side and held the pot to his lips.

"Drink," she said, and he drank. The fluid was steaming hot and had a rich, spicy taste, and green flakes of some herb were thickly scattered over the surface of the fluid. He drank in slow, deep gulps, and the drink was pungent and volatile. It seemed to explode to hot piney vapor the instant it touched his tongue, and the steaming vapor filled his head—he could feel it clear back in his sinuses—and then expanded through his brain until it seemed that his skull was a tight-stretched balloon filled with hot, pungent smoky flavor. His mind, which had been sleepy and blurred, cleared magically. His eyes brightened; blood pulsed through his body, carrying the influence of the magic herbal tea through every portion of his being, until from head to toe he felt tinglingly alive.

She took the pot away, wiped his lips on a scrap of rag; and he looked up into her face and said, "Thyra."

She gasped—it was almost a cry—and all but dropped the earthen pot. A rustle came from behind him, and the old man came shuffling out, wrapped in a blanket. His queue was disarranged, his eyes puffy, and he looked as if he had been asleep.

"What is it?" the old man demanded querulously. "Is he dead?"

The girl looked down at Kadji, immense eyes shadowed with a wondrous, heartbreaking relief.

"He is well . . . *well* . . . he knew me, and called my name . . ."

Kadji was about to say something then, but just at that moment he fell asleep again.

WHEN HE next awoke it seemed to be evening, for no light seeped through the fur across the cave mouth to paint the rocky roof with radiance. Kadji found himself stripped to the waist and the old man—Akthoob, he remembered his name now—was sponging his torso with hot soapy water. He blinked at the Easterling and essayed a sketchy grin. It was a feeble excuse for a smile, and it stretched the skin of his cheeks in such a manner that he guessed it had been rather a long time since he had last smiled, but it delighted Akthoob. The long bony yellow face split in an enormous toothy grin and the slitted black eyes almost vanished.

"This person assumes you are feeling much better, yes?" the old man asked, bobbing and ducking his head happily. Kadji said that he felt fine.

They talked for a little, in a lazy fashion, while Akthoob carefully washed and dried his body and then covered him with soft blankets again. Kadji mentioned something about his dreams, knowing now that they must have been lucid wakeful intervals between coma and fever-spasms.

"I remember one dream," he said vaguely. "Thyra was performing a sort of ritual or prayer over me, and you were shaking your head in a disapproving fashion."

"Ah, yes?"

"Umm. You kept saying something, Zoromesh, that's it; Zoromesh, Zoromesh. I couldn't understand what you meant, nor why the name of Thyra's province should disturb you so . . . it puzzled me for the longest while, in a dim sort of way."

"Ah. Hem. This person suggests that if you are very careful you might roll over upon your honorable face so that your back might be cleansed," murmured Akthoob politely, as if he had not heard. His eyes were evasive, and he seemed distinctly uncomfortable.

"Where are we, anyway, old man?" the boy warrior asked dreamily, while Akthoob sponged his back clean.

"A small cave in the Thirty Hills, ten leagues east of the Perushka encampment. This person and the lady Thyra carried you here in one of the gypsy wains, when you were well enough to travel. The cold, you see. We feared to expose you to it for long . . ."

"I would have thought the Perushka dogs would have slain us all, after I fell," Kadji mumbled sleepily. Akthoob giggled.

"That would have been a very great miracle—this person thinks! The honorable Kadji does not remember, but ere he succumbed to his wounds he slew no fewer than thirty Perushka men . . . the few that were left bundled up their wives and children into the wains and rode off screaming a demon was among them armed with an awful glittering axe!" Akthoob giggled at the memory.

"Did I . . . really slay . . . thirty men?" Kadji mumbled, half asleep. But before hearing the answer he dozed off again, made sleepy by the snug warmth of the cave and the hypnotic rhythm of the old Easterling's rubbing hands upon his back.

But he remembered the word: *Zoromesh;* and he intended to pursue the mystery when next he awoke.

iii. In the Hills

THE NEXT week or so he mended slowly. He did not sleep as much, and they gave him much rare meat to eat, and even a little wine, and he was permitted, after a while, to sit up, to stand, and even to walk a bit, though walking tired him rapidly.

Kadji understood that he had been terribly ill for a long time; so ill that for fifteen straight days he had hovered on the brink of the Dark Kingdom of Death, and the two had labored night and day, sleeping in shifts, fighting to keep him alive.

He assumed it had been Akthoob who had saved him, for he thought a wizard would have knowledge of the healing arts; but no, it had been Thyra. The girl had nursed him with endless solicitude, to the peril of her own health. He felt vaguely surprised that a gently reared Princess of the Blood had such mastery of healing, but he remembered that Zoromesh was famous for its witches—White Witches they were, thinkers and healers, not worshippers of evil—and perchance the girl had learned somewhat of their art in her childhood. Akthoob became very unhappy whenever he raised the question, or mentioned Zoromesh, and when once he let fall a casual word about the White Witches, the old man went pale as parchment and changed the subject so abruptly as to be rude.

Kadji filed this small puzzle away, too, under the heading of Mysteries To Be Explored Later.

He had been ill for two full months. His mouth tightened grimly at the news, and he frowned. Shamad was gone now beyond all hope of finding. There were thousand places in the wide-wayed world in w'

Impostor could have hidden himself, so the Quest, if not actually ended, was at least made futile now. . . .

In those two months the worst of winter had passed, and when Kadji was permitted out of the cave he saw that spring was near. Gnarled old treees and withered black shrubs grew near the mouth of the snug little cave, and bright green buds stirred upon them. And here and there upon the rounded low hummocks of the old hills, where patches of dirty snow were slowly shrinking, green young blades of grass were thrusting up through the bare, scabrous soil. Grey skies and lowering clouds were giving way to clear blue skies and the gusty wind brought the smell of fresh grass and sunshine.

Further east by some leagues was a city and to it they intended, when Kadji was strong enough to ride. They had lived through the winter in the cave, Akthoob and Thyra taking turns at hunting, and the great wolf, Bazan, proving himself the finest huntsman of them all. It had been hard—grim and desperate at times—that winter, but it was almost over.

Every day now Kadji exercised in the sun. He had emerged from the darkness of his long sleep as pale as a sickly child; but weeks of exercise in the sunshine and fresh air put meat on his bones, toughened his weak sinews, and bronzed him with his usual tan.

A tenderness had grown up between the boy and girl. Their eyes met often, and they laughed together much, although they did not speak to one another for the curious shyness that grew between them. Kadji had no experience with women; Thyra was virtually the first woman since his long-dead mother whom he had known on any terms of intimacy. At times Thyra was gay and laughing with him, her face no longer thin and worn, but flushed and bright-cheeked; at times she seemed sad, moody and withdrawn and even abrupt. It was as if she expected something from him, a word, a look, a touch, that would prove the overture to affection. If so, the gesture was not forthcoming, and at times she seemed puzzled and hurt by his lack of response.

Kadji did not understand her feelings at first; he was baffled by her changeful moods, and grew angry sometimes when she was silent with him. He wanted her always to be laughing, always gay and happy. When it dawned on him that she was waiting for him to make an overture, he became most unhappy. It was not that she did not excite and stimulate him, for she did. But he was sworn to a sacred Quest, and a vow of chastity was upon him. In Kadji's zealous and perhaps over-strict interpretation of the meaning of that vow, even a gesture or token of affection was forbidden. For it seemed to him that there was no very great difference between the physical act of love and a tender word or gesture of love: hence his vow forbade him from either.

He grew puzzled that she could not understand this, for surely she knew he bore with him the sacred honor of his people and could not act as he wished. He was not a free agent, but a bound man. Why could the stubborn girl not see this and stop mooning at him one moment and snapping rudely at him the next?

From feeling puzzled he came to feel hurt and from thence to feeling angry with her, and he exhibited a bit of rudeness himself, from time to time. Old Akthoob sighed dismally, seeing the growing gulf of silence and misunderstanding between the young people, and reflected sadly that to be young is to be terribly vulnerable; it was better, he thought, on the whole, to be old and be past such storms and furies.

But the wise old wizard said nothing to either of them. He had his reasons. He suspected a terrible truth about the girl but it was not his secret to divulge. Besides, although he did not think so, he *might* be wrong.

The next morning they awoke to find Thyra g

iv. Ambar

SHE MUST have arisen before dawn, saddled her grey mare, packed her clothing, weapons and provisions, and ridden off with the great plains-wolf loping like a shadowy phantom at her side. She had left no message, no explanation.

Kadji was grimly silent. He had by this time recovered most of his strength and expressed his determination to press on to the town of Ambar which lay further east; there they could pause before deciding whether to continue east on a trail now months old, or give up the Quest altogether.

The old Easterling wizard did not ask why this decision could not be reached here in the hills. He guessed that this cave bore too many reminders of the girl Thyra, too many memories, for Kadji to endure. They rode east on the Grand Chemedis Road under skies clear and fresh and across a world quickening with the green impulse of spring.

Ambar was a squalid huddle of hovels woven through with reeking alleys, dominated by the hulking ruins of a fallen wall and the time-eaten wreckage of a mighty citadel. Once this had been a provincial outpost of the great world-conquering Horde, but that was ages ago, when Chemedis, City of the Kings, had been young and rich and powerful. That age had long-since passed, the two travelers knew, and although a shrunken remnant of the Chemed Horde yet lurked in the half-ruined, half-deserted metropolis of Chemedis itself, many leagues to the east, all of this portion of the vanished empire had been abandoned for centuries and was given over to wilderness.

They found an inn in Ambar where they could stay

and house their steeds, but no one knew aught of any travelers before them. They lingered a time, Kadji grim and sullen, old Akthoob dismal and unhappy, wondering what to do. And then occurred a diversion.

Merchant caravans still used the Grand Chemedis Road, of course. The mighty highway spanned half a continent, and on their year-long journeys between the raw young kingdoms of the west and the ancient and decadent empires of the east, there was no better route than the massive way of paven road that had been constructed in the golden days of the first and mightiest of the great Ja Chans of the Horde.

Some of these merchants were of Akthoob's own people, as their yellow skin, black queues, and slitted eyes attested. During long evenings in the inn of Ambar, the old wizard conversed with his countrymen, and one evening he came to Kadji quivering with excitement.

"It is an odd tale, but this lowly one suggests there may be something of interest therein," he puffed, black eyes a-glitter with suppressed eagerness. Kadji bade him speak on.

The tale was shadowy and elusive, but it hinted at something that made Kadji's blue eyes sparkle. Far to the east, in the half-ruined splendor of Chemedis where the vapid, enfeebled, and powerless descendant of the world-whelming Ja Chans of old held his shrunken court, a mysterious and unknown being had materialized out of nowhere and had rapidly risen to a position of enormous influence. No man knew the history of the nameless one, nor from what dim corner of this world of Gulzund he had come, but he claimed to be a messiah returned from out of ancient time to awaken the weak and languid and decadent Horde to its golden days of former greatness.

Old Chemedian prophecies whispered that a m

would come after ages of time—a Masked Prophet who would rouse the Chemed warriors again, and place the descendant of the Ja Chans upon the world-spanning throne of his ancestors. Kamon-Thaa, the God worshipped by the Hordesmen, would lend him magical powers. And this prophecy had come to pass!

"When did this Masked Prophet appear in Chemedis?" asked Kadji, frowning.

Akthoob told him, and the boy warrior did some quick calculations. The date of the messiah's appearance was about the time Shamad could be expected to have reached Chemedis, had he in fact traveled on into the east, instead of turning back. And it was not unlike the clever opportunist, having won but failed to hold one throne, to gamble for another. . . .

"I suppose it *could* be him," the boy muttered. "But have you any other reason to suspect the Masked Prophet to be our quarry, beyond the mere coincidence of dates?"

Akthoob had indeed. "As proof of his god-given and sorcerous powers, the Prophet goes ever accompanied by a tame and subservient demon . . . a Serpent Demon, this person has been told . . . and Yakthuùl the caravan-master, the source of this information, has seen this strange and hellish monster, and describes him shudderingly as hulking and anthropoid, but glittering in blue scales—"

"—*Zamog!*" Kadji exclaimed. "It must be he!"

Akthoob nodded, a smile of satisfaction on his thin lips.

"So this lowly one surmised," he purred.

v. Caravan Trail

KADJI WAS elated with this clue to Shamad's whereabouts, although it would pose a bit of a problem to pluck his enemy from amidst the court of the Ja Chan. *That* problem, however, they would face when they came to it. But the assumption that the Masked Prophet of Kamon-Thaa and Shamad the Impostor were one and the same man was too logical to overlook, and worth a trip to Chemedis to investigate.

Akthoob arranged passage for his friend and himself with his fellow countryman, Yakthuul, whose caravan was bound east on the Grand Chemedis Road and would pause for a time in the city of the Ja Chan before continuing further east and north to the kingdoms at the world's remote edge. They had little gold left, but Yakthuul could always use a wizard to read the omens and ward off evil spirits, and another warrior handy with axe and sword was always welcome, as there were bandits aplenty who devoted their time to raiding the infrequent but always wealthy merchant caravans. Thus they rode out of the little town of Ambar under a grey and bleak dawn.

Yakthuul the caravan master was fat and sleepy-eyed and rode in a comfortable carriage drawn by the shaggy little ponies of the eastern plains. This was due not only to his fondness for the bodily comforts but because he was too fat to sit astride a horse. Kadji held little converse with the merchant, who had a sort of suave contempt for the raw young kingdoms of the west, and considered Nomads of the plains like Kadji little better than barbarians, devoid of culture or history. But Akthoob was often invited to partake of the merchant princeling's hospitality and came reeling back to the little he shared with the Red Hawk much the worse for liquor, night after night. Yakthuul, it seemed, was given to a potent beverage common in the kingdoms of the east, but unknown in the west. This powerful liquor was distilled from a fruit wine and was a heady intoxicant.

It was on one of these evenings when Akthoob had imbibed a bit more freely than was his wont, that Kadji conceived of a clever plan. The boy warrior thought often of the flamehaired girl, Thyra, and of the mysteries surrounding her, and the enigma of her true identity. He was convinced that the old Easterling wizard knew or suspected her secret, although he concealed it from Kadji and would not divulge it. Thus one chilly night in early spring when they had been riding the caravan trail for two weeks, and Akthoob returned to their tent very much the worse for the potent alcoholic beverage, Kadji got him talking and maneuvered the direction of the conversation toward the girl Thyra and the surprising knowledge of the healing arts she had displayed when he lay ill almost to the point of death from the terrible wounds he had sustained in the camp of the villainous Perushka.

"Odd that a Princess of the Blood should know how to care for an injured man with such skill," he said, when the garrulous and drunken old wizard had begun to talk of Thyra.

"Ah, more than odd, yes," murmured Akthoob sleepily. "This humble person knows little enough of the healing science, but he knows that it is performed with herbs and elixirs, not with . . ." and here he used a word which meant 'the-sending-forth-of-the-soul' ". . . 'twas White Magic the young woman used, not medicine . . . aii, she is not what she did seem to be, although this one cannot guess why she did lie to us. . . ."

It came out slowly that Akthoob suspected Thyra was not the Princess she had claimed to be, but one of

112

the White Witches of Zoromesh! Kadji bit his lips, and murmured more questions into the ear of the sleepy old wizard.

"The honorable youth could not speak of his love for the maiden for his vows forbid it . . . aye, but little did he suspect that the same holds true for the young woman, if indeed she be of the Zoromesh covens . . . *for they are sworn to perpetual virginity.*"

Kadji suppressed a gasp of amazement. Sudden understanding flooded his mind: it was not to be wondered at, that a wall of silence and misunderstanding had risen between him and the girl, forming a breach between them.

He, sworn to chastity for the duration of his sacred Quest, could not display the growing love he felt for the flamehaired girl . . . and she, sworn to virginity by the vows of her sorcerous sisterhood, was equally bound. But—neither had known of the other's vow, and both misunderstood the silence between them for lack of response!

He groaned and bit off a savage curse. O, the folly of it all!

Each, bound by vows which forbade the expression of the affection they felt, had not understood the other to be similarly bound—had not understood why the other had not expressed that affection—had grown hurt, then angry, then bitter.

Kadji put his head in his hands. Thyra was gone and he would not find her again in the wide-wayed world. She would never realize that he, too, felt the stirrings of love. The irony of the dilemma was cruel. But life itself is cruel, as the boy warrior was beginning to discover.

vi. The White Witches

THE NEXT morning they rose, Akthoob with an aching head and a queasy stomach, feebly swearing that never again would he imbibe so freely of Yakthuul's fiery brandy.

They breakfasted over a smoky fire and Kadji confessed that he had pried the truth out of his comrade the night before. Akthoob was glum and dispirited, and not entirely from the after-effects of his drinking the night before. He had hoped to spare the boy's feelings by keeping from him his suspicions that Thyra was an impostor and had lied to them.

Horns blew from the forefront of the caravan, and creaking wains began drawing into line for the days' journey. They hastily crushed out their fire, saddled up, and mounted to join the wagontrain. As they rode in the wake of a huge wain, Akthoob miserably revealed the full weight of his suspicions.

"This miserable person suspects the purposes of the noble young woman, although he has not dared to give words to them ere this," he muttered. "Now they matter not, nor can they deal the honorable Kadji greater hurt than his heart has already sustained."

He then, in his flowery and indirect mode of speech, explained the whole story for the first time.

The wizards and sorcerers and magicians of this world of Gulzund, he told Kadji, are organized into various fraternities and guilds, among them being the White Sisterhood of Zoromesh.

Although his homeland lay very far to the east, in the northern land of Zool which lay above the Yan Than

114

Mountains near the Frozen Country, and though he had not previously visited the world's west, old Akthoob knew by reputation of this Sisterhood.

The motives of the White Witches were shadowy and mysterious, even to their brother magicians. But it was known that from time to time they intervened in the great affairs at the center of the world's stage, for reasons unguessable, and then returned again to the seclusion of their remote and secret sororities. Akthoob had surmised that for some reason the Sisterhood had interested itself in the dynastic troubles of imperial Khôr, and had dispatched the girl Thyra, disguised as a Dragon Princess, to make contact with the Emperor Yakthodah.

But Akthoob could not hazard a guess as to the purpose of her mission, nor did Kadji greatly care.

It was enough to know that she had lied to him.

But the question remained unanswered: was she his friend or his enemy?

True, she had nursed him back to health, which is something one seldom does for a foeman. But that the motive for that action might have been an obscure sense of obligation, since it had been, to some degree, her fault that he had been cut down by the swarthy Perushka rogues in the first place.

Had she been sent to build an alliance of power between the mysterious White Witches of westernmost Zoromesh and the Dragon Throne? Or had it been her purpose to expose Shamad for a rank impostor?

She had told Kadji she meant to expose and thus destroy him, but Kadji could no longer trust anything she had said to be the truth, since she had lied about being a Princess of the House of Turmalin.

And one lie—discovered—throws question on a thousand truths.

He rode on all that day frowning in sullen thought, his mind a weary turmoil of conflicting emotions. If ever they met again, would it be as enemies—or allies?

vii. City of the Ja Chan

THEY PASSED half a moon on the long road into the mysterious and little-known realms of the east, and early summer was come.

Golden Khôr was far behind him now, and the Nomad plains of his people even further remote. He felt lost and alone amidst an unknown world, as if the plainlands that had been his home had become lost in the mists of the far distance.

Now he traveled among a people strange and alien to him: a dwarfish folk with yellow faces, slant eyes and shaven pates, who rode curious shaggy ponies with braided manes and who went garbed in fantastic armor of lacquered and gilded leather, with conical helmets of polished copper. They spoke a strange tongue and worshipped alien gods, and among them, in these strange weird lands of the remote east, he felt very much the stranger.

Akthoob, however, was his constant companion, and during the long days and nights they followed in the train of the mighty caravan of Yakthuul the merchant, the kindly old wizard patiently instructed him in the intricacies of the eastern tongue. It was bafflingly different from the language of the west, but he mastered enough of it to hold at least a halting converse with the bandy-legged little men about him.

It felt odd to Kadji to find himself a stranger, for all his life had been spent among people of his own kind who spoke his own tongue and knew the same ways. He recalled when first he had encountered Akthoob, many

116

months ago and many leagues to the west, in the House of the Seven Moons in distant Khôr. Then the little Easterling wizard had been the stranger; now their positions were reversed, and it was Kadji, with his rangy height, his length of leg, his pale skin and straight eyes and starting thatch of yellow hair, who was the stranger.

He felt lost and alone here on the other side of the world. The world was vaster than he had guessed, and amid its endless leagues, he dwindled to a minute fleck upon a huge and unexplored chart. And his all-important mission, the redeeming of the sacred honor of his clan, dwindled into insignificance and he must be constantly reminding himself of the importance of his Quest. In truth it was hard, for now he moved in a world that had never heard of the Chayyim Kozanga Nomads, and to whom the holy Axe of Thom-Ra, and in verity Thom-Ra himself, were meaningless names. . . .

IT WAS thus, in a mood of alienage and strangerhood, that Kadji came to the king city of the once-mighty Horde, and found the gates of immemorial Chemedis opening before him.

The city was vast and bewildering, but to every hand lay the evidence of an advanced and glorious civilization. Khôr, for all its imperial magnificence, could have been tucked away in one corner of Chemedis and been easily lost.

All of red stone was the old city built, or if not, then the masonry was sheathed in red plaster. The buildings were immense and complicated warrens, almost minor cities in themselves, each crowned with spires and minarets as thickly set as the boles of a forest. The walls of Chemedis were so enormous that entire regiments were housed within them, together with stables and granaries, barracks and kitchens.

The architecture was bewildering in its multiform complexity: great, sleepy-lidded faces of stone gazed down from the eight-sided towers; fantastic dragon-hybrids writhed entangled coils above portal and arch; many-armed and beast-headed gods thronged the paven ways, lining entire avenues in rank on rank of carven stone idols so innumerable as to suggest pantheons as populous as dynasties.

For all its size and splendor, the city was a half-deserted ruin. The entire southern half lay mouldering in decay; kingly mansions were gutted shells; great twisted trees grew in the midst of avenues where once Hordes had marched forth to the conquest of half the world. A once-sophisticated and urban people had degenerated to greasy-faced savages, squatting in filthy hovels built amidst the wreckage of immense palaces their own ancestors had reared. The black oil smoke of cook-fires rose beside ragged tents; naked yellow children ran through paven ways buried beneath centuries of filth; statues lay fallen to fragments; fires had consumed entire suburbs and had burnt out, exhausting their flames against walls of imperishable marble.

Amidst the vast sprawling metropolis rose the Sun Palace, the residence of the Ja Chan. It dwarfed every other structure in all the magnificent city, and it was still an imposing edifice despite centuries of neglect and decay. One entire wing of the enormous palace had collapsed over the interval of ages, and miles of what had once been immaculately tended gardens had been transformed by neglect into an untamed forest, almost a jungle. Kadji and Akthoob strode into the Sun Palace through a portal that reared thirty yards above their heads and into a hall so vast that the eye could not discern the roof thereof. Beggars and shamans camped in the very hall of the monarch, and Kadji saw alcoves that had become reeking latrines, shrines where now unkempt ponies were stabled, and withered crones huddled in filthy tents that had been made out of superb tapestries. The black smoke of camp fires rose here and there amidst the infinity of the colossal hall to add their grime to columns and architraves black with centuries of filth. The squalor and decay was indescribable; the noise and confusion abominable; and the stench beyond words.

The Ja Chan was fat and giggling, painted like a harlot, and covered with flashing gems. He squatted like a huge toad atop a dais covered with priceless carpets, heaped with cushions, over which a golden canopy was stretched. Once that canopy had blazed like the sun and billowed like a cloud; now it was filthy and tattered.

The Ja Chan hardly noticed their obeisance and nodded absently as Yakthuul deposited a silver-bound casket of treasure on the lowest step. He was busy plucking gobbets of some sweet paste from a battered platinum urn with fat, jewelled, dirty fingers, and stuffing them between the rosy painted lips of several beautiful little boys who lolled or squatted nakedly around his cushioned nest. As the boy-concubines giggled and slobbered, licking the sugary paste from his fat hands, Kadji looked away in disgust . . . and promptly forgot the nauseating squalor and license of this degenerate court in a blinding instant of revelation.

HE QUITTED the presence of the toadlike Ja Chan and happily gained the freshness of open air and clean sunlight again. His head was held high and glory shone in his clear eyes,

The dark time was ended; the feverish and worrisome days, the nights of confusion and torment, of mysteries and enigmas. The enigmas were over and done. The shadows that had clustered about him so long, blurring his sense of purpose, darkening the bright clarity of his mission, all these were now dispersed as swamp-mists are driven away by the rays of the risen sun.

He stood tall and heroic under the blaze of the eastern sun, and he was fit and whole again. Pattering along beside him, hands tucked in the long sleeves of his capacious robe, Akthoob chattered with excitement and nervousness, for the scrawny, faithful little Easterling wizard had seen what Kadji had seen there in the shadows of that abominable throne.

For there on the right hand of the Ja Chan of the Chemed Horde had stood Shamad the Impostor . . . and the Quest of Kadji was nearly at its end!

Shoulders back, head high, one hand resting lovingly on the handle of the Axe of Thom-Ra, the boy warrior, Kadji, the Red Hawk of the Chayyim Kozanga Nomads, strode forth under the burning sun of the World's Edge at last to face his destiny.

Or his doom.

Part Five

THE MASKED PROPHET

Cities are fair and kings are proud,
  Princes have wealth to throw away!
Let war's red music ring forth loud:
  A man can die but once, they say!
          —Road Song of the Kozanga Nomads

i. Seven Gold Dragons

THEY LEFT the mighty fortress, Kadji in elation but the little Easterling wizard somewhat dejected. All the way back to the caravanserai they talked, careful that none should overhear.

"This humble one assumes there can be no error?" mused the little wizard. Kadji shook his head, bright locks stirring on the wind.

"None, little man! True, he went veiled, but 'twas not enough to hide his face from me. When he turned his head to speak to the man beside him, the veil moved asunder and I saw it—that red mark on his face that is shapen like a *tarisk* leaf. Lucky for us that birth-blemish is low on his face, below the corner of the mouth, for were it higher the mere stirring of the veil would not have disclosed it. Nay, 'tis him we seek, the Impostor himself!"

The little Easterling grumbled and groused under his breath. When Kadji demanded to know what was troubling him, old Akthoop groaned: "Naught indeed, young sir, save for the slight problem of what we are now to do."

Kadji frowned. "To do? Why, expose the Masked Prophet for an impostor, what else?"

"Indeed? And may this humble and lowly person inquire how the young warrior plans to accomplish that?"

Precisely how to unveil Shamad was a bit of a problem, and Kadji acknowledged that it would take some thought. Just pointing the finger of accusation and crying out "Impostor" . . . well, that would accomplish little. All Shamad had to do, in such an event, was to deny the charge: Kadji had no proof. To recount the story of his Quest thus far would be merely hearsay, and Shamad could lightly shrug it off.

The nexus of the problem was that the Impostor had ascended to a place of tremendous influence and power among the Chemed Horde. Playing upon the superstitious terrors of the barbaric and degenerate Hordesmen, he had won first their fear and then their enthusiastic worship, for it is a short road from superstition to fanaticism. Somehow or other he had managed to strike awe into them, to convince them that he was the mighty Prophet of old, risen from the shadows of death to lead them on to recover the glories of their former greatness.

Akthoob, like all magicians, was a clever practical psychologist. He knew that one way to persuade great masses of men to join your cause was to tell them what they most wanted to hear. Men are easily convinced that what they wish to be true—*is* true. Here, in the decayed wreckage of their past grandeur, the remnants of the gigantic Horde wanted desperately to be told that they had the favor of their savage gods and could recover the world-spanning empire they had lost. For generations they had dreamed that the hallowed Masked Prophet of Kamon-Thaa would someday return to lend his supernatural powers to the restoration of their greatness. Now that he had in fact returned, they would believe in him to the last; were Kadji to force them to face reality and to abandon their dreams of glory, they would trample him down. They did not *want* the truth; they would cling hungrily to their dream and would defend Shamad against a thousand Kadjis!

Back in the caravanserai they discussed the problem over a bottle of tart purpleberry wine while the shadows of afternoon lengthened in the ruin-choked forum outside. And when they came to settle the bill, yet another problem presented itself.

They were growing short of funds.

THE NEXT day they busied themselves seeking some sort of employment whereon to live while they sought a route to their goal. But this proved difficult.

Akthoob might earn a few copper coins performing his magical feats in wineshop or marketplace, but the competition was enormous. Half the sorcerers and magicians of the eastern kingdoms were gathering in the metropolis of Chemedis, for the Masked Prophet was assembling a legion of wizards. When the Horde was ready to begin the reconquest of the world, it would fight with sorcery against the swords of the foe. And thus, in every wineshop, on every street corner, and in each forum or square, a dozen or a score of thaumaturgists were already performing their shadowy arts to entertain the throng of warriors. Akthoob returned to the inn as Kylix the sun star sank crimson in the east, and he returned with scarce enough coppers to afford the cheapest evening meal for the two.

Kadji had met with even less luck. In a city so huge, there should have been many ways in which a strong youth could gain employment—but he had found none. And each person to whom he had applied had turned him away with the same words—"The Masked Prophet has declared that all other occupations save the glorious profession of the warrior are treason against the Sun Throne. In the war of destiny, all men shall be warriors of the Ja Chan!"

"At this rate, we shall be able to afford our room for only another two days, this person fears," moaned Akthoob. "Then we must sell our horses and beg in the streets, if we would not starve. *Aii*, this lowly one should have stayed in golden Khôr!"

Kadji grimly downed the cheap supper of black bread and ale, and determined there was only one

125

course for them to follow. He had not yet figured out a method by which the Masked Prophet could be exposed. He needed more time. And there was only one thing that they could do to buy time.

And that was—sell themselves!

Thus at dawn of the following day, Kadji, Red Hawk of the Chayyim Kozanga Nomads, sold his sword. The emblem of the seven gold dragons was sewn on his tunic, and he became a warrior in the Chemed Horde, a mercenary in the service of the Ja Chan.

ii. *Again, the Flamehaired Girl*

THE NEXT few days passed swiftly. From sunup to evening, Kadji drilled under the merciless eyes of the Horde officers. The Chemed warriors fought from horseback, with pikestaff, hook sword, and barbed lash, and in the use of these weapons Kadji required much drilling. He worked, ate and slept with his fellow warriors, and seldom could find the time to consult with Akthoob; indeed, the little Easterling had enlisted in the corps of wizards and was equally busy during the daylight hours.

Kadji had feared that being an outlander would make him an oddity among the little slant-eyed, bandy-legged Easterling warriors. Happily, this was not true: many a white-skinned Westerling had drifted east to join the growing ranks of the Horde, for the Ja Chan scattered his golden largesse with a liberal hand and the host of the Horde had dwindled so much in recent generations that to build an army for the reconquest of the world he was forced to fill whole regiments with Westerling mercenaries. Indeed, there were thousands of the tall stalwart light-skinned warriors of the west in the streets of

Chemedis, and among them Kadji was but another stranger.

The days passed swiftly and Kadji found little leisure to work on the problem that baffled him, although now as a warrior of the Horde he might find it easier to gain access to Sun Throne when time came to rip the veil from the face of the false Prophet.

All day he labored in the ranks, learning to ride the little shaggy-maned ponies bareback in the Horde fashion; learning to use the hook sword and barbed whip and long-handled pike that were the traditional and sacred weapons of the Chemed Horde warriors. Each night in the crowded barracks he went to his pallet with aching muscles and weary limbs, too exhausted to think and plot and plan, only to fall asleep almost as soon as his head touched the pallet; and the sleeps that followed were deep and dreamless sleeps.

Day by day the host of the Horde grew. Thousands of new warriors swelled the ranks of the Chemed warriors ... Easterling peasants and farmers, the younger sons of noble lords, wandering adventurers and mercenary swordsmen ... they came flocking to the Seven Dragons Banner, drawn by the magic of the legended empire of old and by the glory of the Arisen One, as the Masked Prophet was called.

And then one day Kadji saw her again.

His squadron was riding through the streets to an exercise field on the other side of the barracks area. It was a rainy day, the sky veiled in gloom, high-piled clouds mantling the west, the broken and crumbling pave glistening with puddles. In double file the Westerling mercenaries rode through the streets cloaked and hooded against the wet.

There were few out on so dismal a day, but as they rode along Kadji noticed someone riding a horse that looked familiar.

Even more familiar was the great grey wolf that glided like a shadowy phantom at the side of the horse.

When they drew alongside Kadji strove to catch a glimpse of the rider's face, but it was hooded like his own against the downpour.

But what drew him up tense in the saddle, what forced a cry from his lips, was the glimpse he caught of the rider's hair.

It was red and gold, like flame, that long lock of hair that had escaped from the rain hood.

Long and rippling: a woman's hair.

Thyra's hair!

iii. *The Xin Ritual*

ALAS, HE WAS a bound man now, and not a free agent; thus he must obey the orders of his officer and continue on to another weary day of weapon practice. He could not obey his inclinations and turn aside to investigate this flamehaired woman who rode the streets of ruined and age-old Chemedis with a great grey plains-wolf at her side like a savage dog.

But he could not get her out of his mind! That it was, must be, Thyra, he entertained no doubt. But what was her mission to the court of the Ja Chan?

Had she, like them, discovered that Shamad now posed as the Arisen One, the shadowy and mysterious messiah of old, returned to lead the Horde to the heights of its lost glory?

If so, was she here to destroy Shamad—or to join forces with him? To expose him to the fury of those whom he had hoaxed . . . or to lend him the allegiance and supernatural aid of the White Witches of Zoromesh?

Kadji did not know what to believe. But he feared . . .

ONCE A WEEK, Kadji went off duty and was permitted to leave the crowded barracks and seek an evening's diversion in the wineshops and pleasure-houses of the great metropolis.

On these nights, it was his custom to meet with Akthoob at the caravanserai where their horses were stalled.

On the next such evening they met; a grey evening of cold drizzling rains—the evening of the day he had glimpsed the girl he suspected to be Thyra of Zoromesh in the streets. Kadji was morose, short of tongue, preoccupied. He still could find no way to expose the Masked Prophet for an impostor; although he had found employment and was well-fed and housed, he was no nearer to the solution of his problem and the achievement of his Quest than he had been seven days before. Thus, glumly, he toyed with his wine and stared broodingly into the flames that crackled on the great stone hearth while garrulous old Akthoob chattered merrily.

The little Easterling wizard had found much to seize his interest in the service of the Ja Chan. It was a professional matter, so to speak: the arts and sciences of sorcery were his lifelong enthusiasm, and tonight he was babbling over his new friendship with a necromancer from the isle of Thang in the Southern Sea.

Kadji hearkened to his happy babbling with but half an ear. But he gathered that the prime cause for Akthoob's wizardly enthusiasm was the rarity of his new colleague's specialty. He was given to understand that necromancers were rarely met with in these benighted days, for the ancient science was out of fashion and the necromantic arts were dying and well-nigh lost.

". . . *Aii,* the honorable young warrior doubtless cannot grasp an old man's enthusiasm! But not since this lowly one was a humble young novice in the collegium of the Secret Sciences in far-off Zool below the shadow of Mount Ing, has he chanced to encounter a practitioner of the art necromantic! 'Tis rare in our age to discover one given to the study of this unusual science; ah, but this one hopes to prosper by the gods-given opportunity to gain knowledge of the rare science from this person's new colleague, the Necromancer Arbalac! Perhaps even to observe and experience at first hand the Xin Ritual itself! *That* would truly be a rare intellectual stimulus, for the Xin is, of all the rites of the art of Ceremonial Magic, the most seldom practiced . . ."

"What is a necromancer, anyway?" Kadji grunted. "I thought you were one."

Akthoob's long bony face broke in a toothy smile.

"Ah, young master, surely you jest! This lowly and insignificant one is but a wizard."

"Wizard, necromancer, magician—what's the difference, old man?"

An expression of prim reproof settled on the old Easterling's knobby features.

"What, young sir, is the difference between a blacksmith, an archer, and a raiser of hogs? To each his own art, sayeth the Black Sage! As for the thaumaturgical sciences, the honorable young warrior must know they are several and distinct. A wizard employs talismans and amulets, periapts and sigils—material agents—to effect his sorceries."

"Like the mind-crystal you used back in Khôr, I suppose?" Kadji asked, only half listening.

Akthoob nodded enthusiastically. "Exactly! But a *magician,* now, uses spells and cantrips, mantra, and the speaking-aloud of Names of Power, you see. It is a very different thing: one employs an object, a talisman; the other, a spoken spell or Name."

"And this necromancer of yours? What does he do?"

"*Aii!* A necromancer, now! He conjures up the

spirits of the dead, either to learn from their shadowy lips the secrets of the past, or to gain from the prophecies of the days yet to come. A most difficult art indeed, and far more complicated than the mere casting of a spell—whether by talisman or uttered cantrip! Your necromancer, now, employs *ritual*: the drawing of pentacles, the purifying of the chamber, the burning of the appropriate incense, the recitation of the ceremonial conjuration, the use of the Planetary metals . . . ah, a most difficult art, in sooth!"

"And this Xin Ritual? What is that?" asked Kadji.

Akthoob was bubbling with enthusiasm, rubbing his hands together briskly.

"The most concentrated and powerful of all the necromantic rites of Ceremonial Magic," he said. "For it dispenses with all external instruments of the art (save for the use of the Great Conjurational Circle, of course). The Xin Ritual is an act of the disciplined will, and by it the spirit of a dead person may be conjured at any time, in any place, without all the flummery of asperging, suffumigation, purification, incense, perfume, the use of Planetary metals . . ."

Kadji let the old fellow talk on. But ere long, yawning with boredom, he begged his comrade's pardon, and rode sleepily back to the barracks to report in early.

HOURS LATER he came suddenly to wakefulness. From one state to another he snapped, with no discernible transition therebetween. One instant he was deep in the muddle of a confused and shadowy dream—in the next instant he had sprung erect on his pallet, eyes wide open and staring into the darkness where men snored and mumbled in their sleep.

Could any have seen, in the dense blackness of night, the face of the blond young Westerling warrior who

131

worked and fought and ate and slept amongst them, they would have been amazed at the expression of slack-jawed astonishment and joy that spread slowly across Kadji's features in that moment.

For in one swift instant there had dawned upon his comprehension the answer to the riddle . . . the solution to the problem which for so many days had baffled him.

And he knew of a way to expose Shamad amidst all the host of the fanatic Chemed warriors who worshipped him as the Arisen One.

Expose, and . . . *destroy* him and his influence over the Horde of the Ja Chan for all time!

iv. *The Necromancer Arbalac*

THE NEXT seven days were agony to Kadji, for the hours passed with leaden feet, and he must endure the crawling passage of that much time until again he would be free to meet and consult with the little Easterling wizard in the old caravanserai by the Western Gate.

He passed the time, however, gathering information. Few men are so talkative as soldiers, for beyond their exercises they have little else to do but talk to their comrades when confined to the barracks of evenings. And by subtly guiding the direction of his conversations, Kadji bit by bit gained the knowledge that he desired.

The knowledge concerned the festival days observed by the Chemed Horde warriors, and those festival days when the Ja Chan feasts his chieftains and is entertained by displays of prowess.

Kadji soon learned that one of the great feast days was close at hand. It was called the Feast of the Moon Gods, and on that night the Ja Chan would revel with his lords and courtiers, while jugglers and acrobats, dancing girls and sorcerers would perform for the amusement of the Shadow of the Hand of Heaven and his chieftains.

When the seventh day at last had come, Kadji hurried to the old caravanserai by the Western Gate, and ordered a private room wherein he could talk to Akthoob in privacy. Somewhat bewildered by the boy warrior's intensity of emotion, the little old wizard pattered up the stairs and waited patiently while Kadji locked the door and drew him down to a seat at a small rickety table near the small cobwebbed window where they could talk unobserved.

And then, in a low tense voice, he explained his plan, the daring concept that had occurred to him in his dreams that night in the barracks.

Akthoob rolled back his eyes in terror and his sallow skin went pale at the thought. And yet, as Kadji argued urgently and went into each detail, the old Easterling wizard became calmer and began to realize just how foolproof was Kadji's plan.

But there were several difficulties to be resolved, and not the least of these was the problem of enlisting the technical aid of Akthoob's new friend, the wise old Necromancer Arbalac. The heart of the problem was easily captured in few words—why should the old Necromancer risk danger to himself by lending them his scientific assistance? What inducement could they offer? Kadji chewed over that for a moment, then said, "Perhaps we do not need your friend at all. Perhaps he could teach *you* how to perform the Xin Ritual!"

"Perhaps, but—"

"You said it was simple enough, and involved only drawing a circle."

"Yes, but—"

"It is just a matter of memorizing the ceremonial,

isn't it? Couldn't any wizard or magician or whatever perform the ritual if he knew the ceremonial?"

"Yes, probably, but—"

"Then we don't have to involve your friend at all . . . unless he would like to earn the undying gratitude of the Ja Chan, by helping us expose the cruel and ambitious hoaxer who is playing upon the superstitions and the fanaticism of his warriors in an unscrupulous and ambitious bid for power!"

"*Aii*, but would not the honorable Ja Chan feel, instead of gratitude, the same vengeful fury his warriors will feel when their dreams are exposed as sham, as fabrications, and they are brought to the cruel reality!" whimpered the old wizard plaintively. "Have we not already concluded that sleeping men prefer not to wake, and will visit their anger upon those who rouse them from their rosy dreams of empire?"

"Yes," grinned Kadji, "but the Ja Chan is strong enough to protect us even from the vengeance of the outraged faithful. Why should he, you ask? Because the Ja Chan is—*must* be—conscious of the fact that as the Masked Prophet gains power, the Ja Chan *loses* power! No monarch in all this world enjoys watching an underling grow in influence to a position as high as that to which Shamad the Impostor has ascended. Outwardly, the Ja Chan may regret the extinction of the imperial dreams his deluded followers have worshipped; inwardly, he will be relieved, for it must have occurred to him that Shamad may dream of taking his place upon the Sun Throne. The Ja Chan is a fat, weak, pleasure-loving little man, and much of a fool . . . but he was born to power and even fools are jealous of their crown when they suspect another covets it! You might suggest to your necromantic friend this also: a wonder-worker who exposes the fake powers of another wonder-worker gains in prestige and has a good chance at taking over his position, his power, and his prerogatives. It never hurts an artist, whatever his craft, to publicly prove himself superior to a rival artist!"

DUBIOUSLY, Akthoob carried back to his gifted colleague the arguments and inducements Kadji drilled into him, although in his heart of hearts the timid little Easterling doubted they would work.

As for Kadji, he returned to the barracks of the mercenaries in high hopes, and in a mood of suspense, for it would be many days before he could know for certain whether or not his persuasive talents had been sufficient. It would be the night of the Feast of the Moon Gods before the boy warrior would know for sure whether or not his arguments had worked and his plans would bear fruit.

And he had a lot of work to do before that fateful hour arrived!

v. The Feast of the Moon Gods

FOUR DAYS later, toward the hour at which Kylix the sun star burned like a scarlet beacon athwart the shadowy ramparts of the western sky, the mighty Ja Chan of the Chemed Horde held holy festival in the hall of the Sun Throne in the great Sun Palace of his ancient ancestors.

But once in each three years came that night when all seven of the moons of this world of Gulzund were gone from the night sky and left heaven vacant. During the coming hours of absolute darkness the dreaded Night Demon made his triennial assault on the unoccupied heavens, and only the prayers of the faithful sustained

135

the weakened Moon Gods in their epic battle against the Demon of the Darkness.

Or such was the belief of the Chemed barbarians, at any rate.

On this night, then, it was up to the mortal men of the world to lend what illumination they could to alleviate the reign of the darkness. Ten thousand fat white candles blazed in the mighty palace that loomed like a man-made mountain amidst the colossal wreck of Chemedis. The splendour of this radiance gleamed and glistened on polished marble, agate, lapis, jade and malachite—flashed from golden helms, sparkling rubies, burnished shields of bronze, and naked swordblades of shimmering steel. Bedizened in gaudy silks, a mass of dazzling gems from head to foot, the fat little Ja Chan squatted like a bloated and obscene toad in his nest of cushions atop the broad dais, surrounded by squirming boys from his harem. Pots of incense smoked before him, spreading a cloud of pungent blue vapor through the candle-lit air.

Wine flowed like purple rivers. Smoking meats were laid before the plumed lords of the Chemed Horde in such numbers that the steam of their bubbling gravies thickened the air with succulent odors.

Dancing girls, their slim tawny bodies fully revealed save for a few beads and bangles, posed and postured lithely in the immemorial ceremonial dances. Capering dwarves in fantastic garments clowned and waddled about comically. Jugglers filled the air with spinning balls, ate fire and breathed flames, while acrobats spun through hoops of blazing fire and twisted their bodies into weird positions to escape the glittering slash of naked blades.

All was noise, light, tumult, confusion. From where he stood in the shadow of one colossal pillar, Kadji felt stunned by the riot of sound and color and motion, dazzled by light—light everywhere—flashing, dancing, glittering, beaming from every polished surface and metal mirror.

To bribe those who selected warriors to serve as guards in the Sun Palace, and to make certain that he was one of the chosen, Kadji had squandered every last copper he had earned during all his weeks of service with the Horde.

But it was worth it, for—if all went according to plan—before the east reddened to the coming of dawn, the Quest of Kadji would have reached its end, and Shamad the Impostor would be dead.

From his post in the shadow of the pillar, Kadji stared hungrily upon the person of his adversary. For many months he had fought his way across half the world to bring down the doom of the gods on the beautiful head of Shamad the Impostor. He had suffered the hardships of travel, cold nights spent on the hard earth under star-strewn skies. He had come through battle and siege, treachery and delay, to this hour. His path had been long and wearisome, and it had taken him perilously near to the yawning gates of Death . . . but he had survived, and ere long, he would triumph.

The Masked Prophet sat drinking purple wine and turning his veiled and hidden eyes upon the slim golden bodies of the dancing girls. His tall, strongly built body was robed in priceless silks of mystic green; gems flashed on his hands, which were gloved in black satin; expensive boots of scarlet leather showed beneath the hem of his silken gown. There was no slightest portion of his flesh bare to Kadji's eyes. But the boy warrior knew beyond question that the tall figure in the shimmering robes, his face veiled in shadowy mystery, was Shamad, he who had earlier borne the proud name of Yakthodah. His identity could be seen in the arrogant posture of his body, in the kingly way his proud head was held erect, in the grace wherewith he disposed his limbs.

Silent, hidden among the shadows, the Red Hawk watched his deadly enemy, and beneath his tunic he fondled the handle of the Axe of Thom-Ra.

Now a deep gong rang out, thrilling the vibrant air.

A magnificent chamberlain in silver cloth and ebon velvet raised his plumed staff and boomed out!

"The magicians are come before the glory of the Sun Throne, to perform their arts of mystery before the Ja Chan!"

And hidden in the shadows, Kadji caught his breath in sudden fear.

What if Akthoob had failed to persuade Arbalac to perform the ritual?

What if Arbalac had been unwilling, either to perform it himself, or to instruct Akthoob in the art?

If that were the case, then all Kadji's plans had gone for nothing . . .

His heart in his mouth, the Red Hawk of the Chayyim Kozanga searched the file of robed magicians with eager, fearful, expectant eyes.

vi. *The Spectre*

THERE WERE plump, placid-faced sorcerers from Quarah and Dhesh who struck the paven floor with long staves and, lo! flames of emerald and ruby and gold sprang from cold stone to dance and coil and slither to the weird song of unseen flutes.

There were gaunt magicians from Shoth Am and the Mountain Countries, spirit beads wound about their bony brows and dangling in clanking chains from thin bare wrists. They sang complex spells and the rolling clouds of incense became fields of shimmering color whereon could be seen depicted the Ja Chan at the head of his tremendous Horde marching across the face of Gulzund in victory and triumph, his scarlet sword hidden, from hilt to point, in crowns, crowns and tiaras and coronets.

There were dwarfed wizards from Orome and the White River Kingdoms, small smiling men with agile glittering eyes, their narrow beards stained blue, their mouths reddened with *jayol*. They set at the compass points sigils of the Planetary Metals, gold discs for Zao, iron plates for Thoorana, lead rondules for Olymbris, cirques of silver for Zephrondus. Then, brandishing talismans that flared in glimmering haloes of mystic fire, they raised spirits and summoned down demons from the stars to relate, in deep sepulchral voices, of the marvels of the universe.

Then stepped forth a tremendous man in robes of glorious scarlet. He was immense, taller than a Barbarian, and of more mighty girth than the fattest of men. He must have weighed three hundred stone or more. His round, shaven face glistened with sweat, and he wheezed and puffed at the exertion of moving his massive weight.

The chamberlain's steel mace rang against the broken pave as he summoned attention for the next practitioner of the magic arts.

"The Necromancer Arbalac from the isle of Thang in the Southern Seas will perform a rare and unusual feat of the art necromantic for the glory of the Ja Chan!" boomed the chamberlain. Kadji tensed in the shadow of the column, relief and new excitement surging through him.

From his girdle the huge Necromancer drew a black wand tipped with a strange grey gem. He uttered a portentious syllable and the gem spluttered into blinding blue fire. With this blazing point Arbalac traced a great

139

circle on the stony pave. The spluttering blue flame left a charred black mark clearly visible on the pave. This, Kadji knew, must be what Akthoob had named the Great Conjurational Circle.

In a deep base voice, the Necromancer spake.

"If the Glorious One will indulge this person for a moment, I shall attempt to summon from the shades of the Kingdom of the Dead the spectre of one who has lain among the shadows for a thousand years," he announced, bowing ponderously in the direction of the Sun Throne. On the dais, the Ja Chan nodded absently, busily fondling one of his painted boys who squirmed and giggled lasciviously under the subtle movements of the jewelled hands.

The black circle lay on the stone floor. At one edge thereof stood the immense figure of the Necromancer, swathed in voluminous robes of arterial crimson. He folded his hands over the black wand. His lips moved without speech. His eyes sank into his head; his face paled and became wet with perspiration. He trembled throughout his ponderous body as if in the grip of some intense emotion. Kadji knew that the Necromancer was concentrating his will to such a degree that by the sheer power of mind alone he could summon into the land of the living an apparition from the Kingdom of Death.

The hall grew still, all watched the gigantic figure in glowing crimson. The iron force of the Necromancer's will seemed to seize and hold the attention of the revelers. Men turned from drinking, feasting, love-making, to stare at the huge bald man.

From his high place, the Masked Prophet turned to watch the Necromancer Arbalac with close attention. Did he feel the icy breath of foreknowledge? Did some eerie premonition of what was about to occur visit his mind with fear?

Within the black circle a shadow began to form.

140

At first it was as tenuous as a wisp of smoke. Gradually, it took on shape and substance as if it gathered weight and being out of the smoky air itself.

It was the likeness of a tall thin man with a gaunt skull and cavernous eyes, swathed in tatters of rotten graveclothes.

The beard of the apparition was long and shaggy and unkempt. Its face was lined with age or sorrow, but its eyes glittered like black cold stars under hollow brows. Some emotion akin to anguish seemed to twist its narrow, lipless mouth into a frozen grimace. Skeletal hands were clasped before its bony breast, which heaved with some terrible emotion.

When at last the spectre had taken on form and substance, the Necromancer relaxed his frightful concentration. He sucked air into starved lungs and gasped, wiping his dripping brow on the sleeve of his crimson robes. Then he peered at the silent figure which loomed within the black circle.

"Speak, phantom, and reveal to us your name," he said in a deep voice.

The hall was deathly silent now. Not a single figure stirred or spoke. The assemblage seemed hardly to breathe. All eyes were fixed on the gaunt, horrible figure of the dead man within the circle.

"Speak, I command you!" Arbalac repeated. "How long has it been since you died? What is your name and condition? *Speak!*"

In a quavering, reedy voice, the spectre made its reply. "A thousand winters have passed over this world of Gulzund since I last dwelt among the living," the thing answered slowly. "For a thousand years have I wandered the cold halls of the restless dead, despairing of my sins, begging for the benison of my gods . . . but now another cry wells up from the center of my soul . . . a yearning for *vengeance* possesses me! Aye, vengeance!

For there is one here among you living men that has done sin against me, and a sin whose depth and consequence you mortal men cannot comprehend!"

Abralac leaned forward, eyes glinting in the candle-glare.

"Who is it that has offended you? Speak, phantasm! Who art thou, and who is that man who has committed evil against one dead for so many generations?"

The spectre unclasped its hands. One arm shot out, drifting through the murk of roiling incense. Gaunt as naked bone was that arm, and tattered ribbons of rotten cloth swung and swayed from it.

The bony finger pointed directly at the place whereupon sat the Masked Prophet. The Prophet sat rigid, unmoving, frozen; his gloved hands clenched the arms of his chair so tightly it seemed almost that the stone would be crushed.

The voice of the spectre rose to an unearthly screech screech of rage and detestation.

All eyes turned to watch the Prophet.

The phantom screamed—

"That man has stolen my very name . . . *for I am the Masked Prophet of Kamon-Thaa who died a thousand years ago!*"

vii. *The Flame Globe*

SHAMAD SPRANG to his feet and behind him the burly, blue-scaled form of his monstrous henchman also rose, snakelike eyes glittering with cold malice.

On the dais, the Ja Chan sat motionless, his rouged and painted face a mask of utter astonishment.

The taut silence that had gripped the hall while the spectre spoke ceased when Shamad sprang to his feet. It was as if by his sudden movement he had broken the spell that had long held the glittering and barbaric assemblage bound. They roared in one shattering crescendo of red rage. Tables went crashing over, swords were drawn in a hiss of steel against leather, shouting men sprang up yelling for blood.

By his involuntary motion it seemed that Shamad had flinched from the accusation thus leveled at him from the very halls of the dead. If he had remained unmoving —if he had laughed—perhaps he could have retained his grip on the beliefs of the Horde chieftains. But the way he leaped to his feet had, somehow, betrayed his guilt. In an instant the Horde warriors realized how greatly they had been duped. Savages beneath their veneer of civilization, they roared for the blood of the Impostor. In an instant the great room was a shambles. Wine lay spilt in spreading gouts, staining the marble pave with pools of scarlet, like blood. Platters of steaming meats went clanging to the floor and were trampled underfoot by angry men, blind with primal fury.

Upon the great dais of the Sun Throne the Ja Chan still had not moved or spoken. His face bore no expression at all, but in his little pig-eyes, as they looked upon Shamad, appeared a glint of relief and—*amusement!*

It was even as Kadji had prophesied—no king willingly shares one jot of his power with another. Not even with the holiest of priests or prophets.

Cold little eyes glinting with cruel satisfaction, the Ja Chan watched the downfall of him who had pretended to be the Masked Prophet of Kamon-Thaa.

AS FOR Kadji, he had been ready for the moment of his triumph. Even as the first enraged Hordesmen had surged for the chair whereby the false Prophet still stood, the lithe figure of the Red Hawk of the Chayyim Kozanga Nomads had hurtled to their front. From

143

under his uniform tunic he brought forth the Axe of his God and brandished it high.

In the light of ten thousand candles, the Axe of Thom-Ra flashed blindingly as a slice of sun.

And, of all those gathered in that hall, only Shamad recognized it.

The dais whereupon rose the chair of the Prophet towered high above the hall, almost as high as the Sun Throne itself. Six steps led to the summit of the dais where Shamad and Zamog stood facing throng of angry men howling for bloodthirsty vengeance.

Kadji was the first to reach the foot of that dais and as he went leaping up to where Shamad stood he lifted his young voice in a great cry.

In all that place, only Shamad knew the war challenge of the Chayyim Kozanga when he heard it bayed forth.

In a flash—in an instant—Shamad realized how he had been tricked, and by whom. Oh, doubtless he did not know the name of Kadji Red Hawk, but the pale stern features of the boy warrior, his shock of sunny hair, the fierce exultation in the clear gaze of the youth, told Shamad all he needed to know.

They say on the plains that the vengeance of the Kozanga Nomads has an arm long enough to reach from World's Edge to World's Edge. In this swift moment, Shamad realized the truth of that saying, as he stared down frozen into the hawk-bright eyes of Kadji and saw the Sacred Axe glitter through the smoky air as it flashed to sever his throat.

But Shamad the Impostor had been raised in a hard school. They who live by their wits alone—by lie, deception, and deceit—learn early to ward against every turn of the dice or do not survive. And Shamad had survived tighter traps than this. From amidst the very stronghold of his foes, in golden Khôr, he had eluded

144

the assassin's blade, the watchful eye of the plotters, and the armed hosts who would cut him down, to slink forth in secret when all men thought him safely dead.

As the Axe sped for his throat Shamad touched gloved hands together and then stretched them wide, uttering a guttural Word. From charmed sigil rings which had met when his hands were pressed together—sparks of supernal fire flashed!

Floating in thin air between his parted hands appeared a spinning globe of white fire!

Brilliant beyond a thousand suns it blazed! Scorching rays seared deep into Kadji's eyes—he cried out, squeezing shut eyes which watered now from the stab of agony that bit through his very brain. It was as if fiery needles were suddenly thrust through and through his head.

His charge wavered and failed. He lurched to one side, stumbled, and fell.

The flame globe floated up over the throng—and burst!

Light—light—intolerable *light* drenched the hall of the feasting.

And then the darkness came down on them all. Black and deep, as if the ten thousand candles that flared this night to aid the Moon Gods against the Darkness Demon had blown out.

And the hall was filled with men who cursed and cried out and staggered and stumbled, blundering into each other and into the furniture.

They were all struck blind.

viii. Night of Doom

THE TOUCH of the wet rag was soothing to his aching eyes. Kadji huddled against the alley wall and drew in sobbing breaths as the old Easterling wizard bathed his red and bleared eyes with cold water. Old Akthoob made soft, clucking sounds of sympathy as the boy warrior sobbed raggedly.

"So close . . . so very close! *Agh,* Mother Chaya! He was . . . within my grasp! . . . Gods . . . another moment more," the youth wept.

All around them surged the sound of tumult and battle. Several buildings were aflame and corpses hung from rude, improvised gibbets at the head of every street. Rioting had spread through the capital all night long. Men said the treasury had been sacked—the Ja Chan still lived, but had withdrawn into the inner citadel of his palace to consult with the Gods, leaving the city to his roaring warriors who were drunk on the wine of fury and howled for blood like ravening madmen.

Most men within the city had been struck temporarily blind in that same terrible instant the Flame Globe leaped from the hands of the false Prophet.

Driven mad by the sacrilege of the Impostor, tormented by the agony of their seared and sightless eyes, the Hordesmen had gone wild, rampaging through the streets slaying all whom they encountered. As the hours of night crept on toward morning, it was learned that the magic darkness was a passing thing. But even this did little to assuage the wild drunken fury of the deluded warriors. As Shamad had been an outlander, a white-skinned Westerling, some had seized upon the notion that the imposture was a Westerling plot. This had been shouted out, and it had been like a lighted match touched to a lake of oil. The Horde chieftains had come boiling out of the palace roaring against treason and treachery, thundering through the barracks of the Westerling mercenaries to burn and slay.

The Westerlings, struck blind by the same magic, had fought back, thinking their own blindness the magic of the treacherous Easterlings. Blind armies locked in furious battle had crushed and howled through the streets, slaughtering each other in their madness.

Now buildings were seething infernos and streets were choked with rubble, with hasty barricades, with sprawled and crimson-splashed corpses. The black sky was crimsonly underlit with the glare of flaming palaces.

And thus it was that the vain imperial dreams of the Ja Chan died in one terrible night of slaughter and madness and destruction. Even if he survived the riot, his throne intact, the Ja Chan could not again dare dream of his lost empire. . . .

OLD AKTHOOB gently dried Kadji's wet eyes and applied a soothing ointment from his sachel.

Exhausted, his emotions drained, Kadji huddled like a bundle of soiled rags against the alley wall, staring wearily at the dawn-smudged sky.

The agony of blindness had passed. He could see, although it would be days before his tortured eyes regained once more the hawklike fierceness they had known. Somehow, although as blind as he, the old Easterling wizard had gotten the sightless and trampled boy out of the riot-torn palace and to a safe haven. Kadji laid a hand on the old man's shoulder by way of thanks.

"And . . . Shamad?" he asked tiredly.

"Gone . . . gone. Vanished into the night, no man knows how or whither," Akthoob sighed.

"So the road goes on," Kadji whispered.

"Aye."

"Will I ever bring him to swordpoint? Will he always elude my vengeance with his clever tricks?" the boy wondered dully.

The old man chuckled.

"He has not much farther to run, young sir, so this humble person dares to suggest the noble youth will set his back against the wall at last, ere long. For naught lies beyond here save for the measureless sands of a great waste . . . waves of desolation like a bitter and lifeless sea that wash across the leagues to break at last at the world's very Edge! Beyond World's Edge even the cunning Impostor cannot go. . . ."

"I wonder," said Kadji.

"It is truth, young sir. But come! It is death to linger here now that men are beginning to recover from their blindness. The Hordes are slaughtering all Westerlings this night. We must be up and on our way . . . this cowl will mask your white skin from any suspicious eye . . . we must forth to the inn for our ponies, and thence from the gates of Chemedis, and forth on the track of the Impostor before the world's an hour older."

AND THOSE things were done, and as Kylix the sun star rose up over the Edge of this world of Gulzund the two adventurers rode forth from the broken walls of Chemedis into the morning.

Far ahead of them some where rode Shamad, accompanied by his monstrous servant.

And one other rode fast and far. For hard on the heels of the fleeing Impostor rode a young girl with flamegold hair, mounted on a great horse, with a grey plains-wolf loping by her side.

For Thyra alone had observed the flight of Shamad. Perhaps the magic powers invested in her by the White

Witches of Zoromesh had been strong enough to shield her from the blinding beams of the Flame Globe. At any rate she had seen the false Prophet and his dragonish henchman as they fled into the early dawn, and the flamehaired girl had followed not far behind.

This was not known to Kadji.

Neither was it known to Shamad.

But they were destined to meet together, all of them, at World's End.

Part Six

THE ROAD TO WORLD'S END

Ah, it must be a pleasant thing,
  To drink and feast the night away!
But we with empty bellies sing,
  And ride all night—to fight all day!
            —Road Song of the Kozanga Nomads

i. Scarlet Eyes

THE HILLS rose, rounded hummocks of grey earth, like the knees of giants, and beyond them to the east, like the giants themselves, huge humped mountains thrust up athwart the sky. They were old and tired, those mountains, and the wind and weather of millions of years had worn their sharp spires and bladelike crags to smooth rondures.

The mountains marched from north to south, cutting across the drear wastes that lay to the east of Chemedis, and they made an all but impassable barrier to any traveler who dared to venture further east than this. But the flamehaired girl had traversed many thousand leagues of the world on the track of Shamad the Impostor, and mere mountains were not enough to stop her now.

Twilight was falling; the sky darkened slowly. She tugged at the reins and turned the nose of her steed about and thumped her heels in the horse's ribs to spur the weary stumbling steps. Night must not take them here in the waste; higher up in the mountain country they could perhaps find shelter from the creatures which rumour whispered dwelt about and made the night hideous with their cries.

The old, worn map she had borne with her all the way from Zoromesh on the other side of the world, and which still lay folded and tucked in her sash, told of a safe pass through the wall of mountains that marched down from the ultimate pole. The Khondru, it was called. From here she could almost see it, a notch cut by the Gods in the granite wall that locked the east away behind the frowning ramparts of worn old stone.

At the heels of her steed the great plains-wolf loped, but he too was very weary. His tongue hung from between open, panting jaws, and his plume of a tail dragged in the dust. But he did not desert her side: like a gliding phantom, silent as a grey shadow, the wolf slunk after her, lambent eyes of gold flame blazing through the murk of dusk.

She took an ancient track that rose slowly toward the mouth of the pass, winding between the rounded hills. The mare cantered along slowly, lathered and weary. The girl, Thyra, was weary too, aye, bone-weary with hard riding, but she could not let them rest—not here— not yet.

The world darkened around them. The road lifted under them, and the Khondru grew larger till it loomed mighty through the dusk, like the portal of some unknown world, pillared with darkness.

Beyond the pass the plain stretched away east to the Edge of the World. There was naught to see, for night was upon them now and the first of the Seven Moons of Gulzund trembled on the edge of the sky, an orb of dim opal light.

Thyra made camp in the foothills beyond the world-separating range of mountains. She gathered dry dead brush and touched it to crackling flame with a Word she had learned in young girlhood from the White Witches of her homeland. The wickerwork pannier slung across the withers of the grey mare held provisions for many days, dried meat and rank green cheese, black coarse bread and a strong dark wine that had honey in its heart and left the taste of forgotten summer on her tongue.

Wrapped in a fringed and hooded cloak, huddled near the fire for warmth, Thyra munched down bread and cheese, sharing the meat with Bazan the grey wolf. Behind her back, warm and breathing hoarsely, the mare crunched and mumbled its portion of grain.

Even in Chemedis, Thyra had taken precautions of keeping fresh foodstores packed and ready against the need for immediate departure. She knew the wily and cunning ways of Shamad the Impostor; thrice he had eluded her ere this. He had a talent for slipping away suddenly from the center of things; she had resolved that never again should he catch her napping and unprepared.

Finishing her rough meal, the young girl leaned back against the haunches of the mare and stretched out her booted legs wearily, drinking the dark honeyed wine. Thinking of Shamad made her think of Kadji. She wondered what had become of him. She remembered everything about him, his clear and fearless blue eyes, his shock of bright gold hair, the warm tenor of his voice, the way his eyes crinkled when he grinned, the sound of his laughter. Her face expressionless, the flamehaired girl thought back over the list of days to the time he had come to her rescue on the plain, joining the fight against the wolves in the whirling snow . . . and how gloriously he had battled against the villainous treachery of the Perushka at the ambush after leaving golden Khôr. . . .

Her smoky, amber-flaked eyes fathomless, the girl brooded, staring deep into the crackling flames of her small fire.

Kadji . . . Kadji!

She remembered the clean-limbed strength of his young body when she had tended him during the dark time in the cave when he hovered on the brink of death and only her witch arts had stood between the Nomad youth and the Great Shadow. She had handled his body with hands tender yet impersonal, cleansing him, tending to his bodily needs as he lay helpless, raving . . . her Vows she had kept ever in mind during the proximity forced upon them by the smallness of the cramped cave and the cold inhospitality of winter . . . but she was very young and she was very much a woman, and she could not shut out of her mind and heart the strong young manhood of him, or the masculine beauty of his body.

She thought of him now with an odd mixture of tenderness and stubborn anger, remembering how he had seemed to spur her timorous, tentative advances. She had been half a traitor to her own Vows in allowing herself to think of him as a woman though of a man ... surely, *he* had no such soul-sworn oaths to restrain him from thinking her desirable! But he had spurned her overtures coldly and without interest ... *Kadji!*

These thoughts, burning through her heart, made her ignore the sudden stillness of Bazan at her side, and the sudden tension in the air, until the grey wolf growled. She looked up into the cold, cruel eyes of scarlet flame that glared down at her from the black form that towered up against the night.

ii. The Captive

HE WAS all packed and ready and eager to be gone. In his urgency, Shamad begrudged even the little interval of time during which they had rested and eaten and fed the horses. He paced up and down beside the small fire, impatiently flicking his boots with a riding-crop, turning his coldly handsome face to the darkness beyond at every fancied stir or movement.

Flight had become a way of life to him now; but soon —very soon—he would no longer have to flee. Shamad smiled at the thought and stood motionless, gaze turned inward as if contemplating a golden future. Even in repose he betrayed himself, however. A small nerve jumped at the corner of his mouth, and there were lines of strain etched about his eyes. Those eyes had the fixed glare of a madman, inwardly consumed, burning. His wild eyes, stark in the tragic beauty of his perfect features, formed a fearful contrast. Even motionless, his body as well seemed to strain in tension.

"Lord?"

The deep sibilant voice spoke from the dark shadows beyond the circle of light shed by the campfire. Shamad snarled a curse—turned his wild haggard eyes toward the source of the voice—then stiffened again as he saw what his slave had found.

The Dragonman knelt and lay Thyra's body on the sand. Her face was white and still, like a mask of carven alabaster. The flame of her hair lay about her thickly, glowing with burnished highlights in the fire's illumination. Shamad mouthed an obscene word and bent to look more closely at the girl who lay dead or unconscious.

Zamog had brought the horse as well. The mare's eyes rolled nervously, showing the whites, and it snorted and tugged, trying to drag its reins from the grip of the manlike thing that held them. Perhaps the mare's velvet nostrils found the snaky odor of his monstrousness repulsive.

Shamad looked the girl over, eyeing the firm rondure of her proud young breasts. They rose and fell, straining the fabric of her tunic, as she breathed shallowly. She yet lived, it would seem.

He barked a query at the Dragonman.

"Where?"

"In the foothills, some ways behind us. There was a dog or wolf with her but it feared me and fled away in the night," the scaly monsterling said solemnly.

The Impostor grunted. "What of the warrior boy and the old wizard?"

Zamog shrugged, a heaving of broad, apeish shoulders. Firelight glinted on the edges of his scales. His body was entirely scaled, like a serpent, but the scales were different in size and texture. Those on his back and shoulders and upper chest were broad horny plates, tough and thick. They narrowed to fine-grained texture on his face and belly and throat.

"No sign of them, and from the tracks in the sand, they did not accompany her. I wish I could have killed the dog . . ."

"I wish you had, now it has gotten away and may find the others," Shamad said coldly. "They will know something is wrong, for the brute would not willingly have left her side. Odd that it did not fight you."

The blunt-nose, slope-browed face of the monsterling was inscrutable, scarlet eyes inhuman and feral in the glow of the fire. "Dogs do not like me," he grunted slowly. "Something about me strikes them mad with terror . . ."

"Your smell, I suppose," said Shamad carelessly. "Well, at least you were wise enough to take the horse. We can use it to carry our gear, and we can use whatever provisions the girl had with her . . . what did you do to her anyway?"

The monster man shrugged and spread blunt-clawed hands wide.

"She did not move after she saw me. I think terror froze her at the sight of me. So I struck her at the base of the neck and she fell. I was afraid she would cry out and warn the others, for I did not at first realize they were not near. I did not kill her . . ."

Shamad smiled fleetingly. "A good thing you did not! Or I would have made you suffer pain, as I did that time you slew the old noble to get his keys. Do you remember how I bound you to the post and hurt you with hot coals?"

The monsterling's eyes were dull and opaque, and his voice was heavy and lifeless. "I remember."

"Very well; keep it in mind, and do not harm the girl. We shall take her with us."

Zamog stirred uncomfortably.

"Why do we need the girl?" he inquired.

Shamad laughed. "*You* do not need her, but I do! I have not had a woman in many weeks. Also, if the others catch up with us, we can use her as hostage. The boy warrior is chivalrous and noble of heart . . . I think he would not like to see me do to the girl what I did to you that time with the burning coals. I think he will lay down his sword and let me take him, to spare her the pain. Then you can kill him—as slowly as you wish!"

The Dragonman flexed his massive hands slowly.

"I like to kill men," he said thoughtfully.

"I know you do, you ugly beast!" Shamad laughed. "It gives you the same pleasure that I take from women, I have often thought. Well, we are wasting time. Pleasures can come later . . . I would like to put a league between myself and that Nomad boy before day breaks. Saddle up, and put the girl behind you. Bind her wrists together at your belly so she cannot get free when she awakens. And let us be gone, for the love of the Gods! These hills are not healthy at night."

A few moments later they rode on. The fourth moon was above the horizon by now and the desert beyond the low humped hills was awash in hazy shifting shadows. The young moon peered down with cold curiosity as the man and the monster and their captive rode straight across the soft sands into the east and vanished slowly from the sight of any eye but hers.

iii. Bazan

THE OLD Easterling wizard was brewing herb tea over the small fire, stirring the steaming fluid in a small iron pot with a long-handled spoon of carved horn and sniffing in the rich aromatic fragrance with sleepy pleasure when the thing came out of the darkness toward them.

They had ridden hard, to the edge of their horses' endurance, and a while ago they had made a rude camp amidst the waste. Now they had eaten and, while old Akthoob brewed his tea, the boy Kadji rested, sprawled out on his blankets, using the saddle as a sort of pillow. Behind him in the lengthening shadows, his black Feridoon pony and the old wizard's steed munched dried grain from leather feedbags.

The first two moons had just arisen to tremble like orbs of magical colored light on the dim horizon, when the shadowy shape came without a sound out of the blackness of night to stand before them.

It was a great grey shaggy brute with scarlet, lolling tongue and glistening white fangs, and it was enormous —almost as big as the young Nomad warrior himself.

Akthoob uttered a hocked squeal and knocked his herb tea, pot, spoon and all, into the small turf fire.

Kadji sprang to his feet, snatching at his weapons. Then he stayed his hand, for the shaggy grey animal was not making any signs of attack. And it looked familiar. . . .

He stared into the lambent golden eyes of the creature and whispered a name, "Bazan!"

The grey plains-wolf whined deep in his throat and wagged the shadowy plume of his tail, for all the world like a gigantic dog.

"Kill it—kill it!" old Akthoob squeaked, fluttering his bony hands nervously as if hoping to shoo the wolf away. Then he paused, blinking owlishly at the beast, which had padded over to kneel at Kadji's feet. Akthoob sucked in his breath between his teeth with a little whistling sound as, greatly daring, the boy warrior bent slowly and scratched his fingers deep in the thick coarse fur that grew behind the wolf's pointed ears.

The long pink tongue came lolling out and timidly licked the boy's wrist.

"It *is* Bazan," said Kadji slowly, trying to keep the tense excitement out of his voice. "It *must* be! The plains-wolves do not roam these far wastes at the World's Edge . . . and if it is not Thyra's pet, why should a strange plains-wolf be so friendly . . . or be here at all, a thousand leagues and more from the habitat of his own kind?"

Akthoob blinked nervously, but was forced to admit that the beast bore much resemblance to the tame wolf who had followed the flamehaired girl.

"It knows the smell of my body from the weeks we dwelt together in the cave, that time I lay sorely injured and close to the black gates of Death," the boy reasoned. "It knows me for a friend—but why has Bazan left the side of his mistress?"

The old Easterling wizard cleared his throat with a dry cough. "This humble person might suggest that, uh, the honorable lady has met with an accident . . . some enemy, perchance . . ."

The firelight flared in Kadji's eyes. He chewed restlessly on his knuckles.

"You may be right, old man. Shamad is somewhere in this waste of dreary sand . . ."

"Ay, young sir! But it need not be him we seek has harmed or captured the flamehaired one. There are beasts haunt these desolate wastes at the World's Edge. Aye, and the shades of long-dead men roam the shadowy margins of the world, if old tales be true . . ."

"Well, whatever has become of Thyra, her wolf will lead us to where she lies," the boy warrior said. If hurt or—or—slain," the youth gulped, choking a little on the word, "Bazan will guide us to the spot. And if taken captive by Shamad or by some other, the wolf will aid us in tracking her and her captors, as he can follow her scent."

Old Akthoob wearily agreed. "But on the morrow, surely! These old bones ache from hours in the saddle, and the horses are worn to their limit and must rest!"

Reluctantly, Kadji permitted himself to be persuaded, although every fibre of his hot young heart urged him to ride forth into the night on the trail of the flame-haired girl. But he knew it was not a wise course, for if pressed beyond their endurance, the steeds would founder and they must thence forward attempt the crossing of the waste afoot, which were very great folly.

They slept that night rolled in thick blankets beside the guttering fire, and rose with first dawn to eat hastily and ride on toward the Rim of the World.

All that day they rode, with Bazan loping ahead, nose to the ground, guiding them due east. Every two or three hours they paused to rest the horses, and Kadji bitterly begrudged every lost moment. All that day, and much of the night, and for most of the day that followed they rode ever onward, close on the trail of Thyra, and of Shamad the Impostor, too, although they could not be certain of that fact.

As they rode, the little old Easterling wizard grew more and more discomforted. For it looked as if the trail was leading them due east across the world and straight to the gates of Ithombar, king city of the Immortals, whose lofty purple towers were said to rise on the world's ultimate Edge, and which was forbidden to all mortal men by the Gods.

iv. The Chase

THYRA WAS more frightened than she could recall ever having been in all her life. True, she had been frozen with fear when the hulking form of the weird monsterling had loomed up out of the darkness and had strode for her, scarlet eyes gleaming. But that had merely been the natural fear of being attacked and injured, and she would have felt the same feeling had it been a mindless savage predator come loping from the gloom of night's darkness to assault her, and not the Dragonman who served the Impostor.

It was Shamad himself who struck cold terror deep into her soul. Something in his icy, tense, beautiful face, something in the mad flame that burned ever in his fixed, glaring eyes, and something in the tension wherewith he held himself, and the harsh note of hysteria that rang ever in his voice, and most of all in his high-pitched, dreadful laughter—*this* was the thing that filled her heart with the cold, sodden ashes of fear.

Since Zamog the Dragonman had captured her, neither he nor his master had offered her any harm. She was kept bound at all times, her hands tied behind her back when in the saddle, and her legs tied when they slept, and she was completely helpless, save perhaps for her witch powers, which came and went, fickle and untrustworthy, and which could not really be counted upon. If anything, the two males ignored her most of the time, seldom spoke to her, and when a need of the body demanded her attention, it was the blue-scaled monsterling who grudgingly assisted her. She felt no embarrassment or shame under his cold, inhuman eyes, for he was little more than a beast to her mind, and his strange species and her own were so far apart in the spectrum of life that his presence at her ablutions offended her no more than would the presence of her horse or of Bazan, her wolf friend, have given her offense.

But Shamad she feared to the depths of her being, with an icy, heart-stopping terror mingled with a helpless loathing that was indescribable. Partly, this was due to the dread of a normal and healthy mind helpless in the hands of one who was clearly insane. And in part, it was because she knew that he desired her.

For if Zamog regarded her with the aloof, impersonal eye of a beast, Shamad thought of her as a very young and a very desirable woman. She was, of course, a virgin—her youth would have made that certain, even without her Vows as a White Witch of Zoromesh. She was ignorant of adult relations and innocent of their physical aspect, but she had a woman's instinctive knowledge of them, and all the dread and terror of a young girl helpless in the captivity of a man. She avoided the presence of Shamad—avoided even looking at him as much as was possible, fearing to catch his eye—but she was horribly aware that his staring eyes rested meditatively on her very often, and that his gaze lingered on the slim, firmly rounded lines of her strong young body, on the rise and fall of her firm young breasts, on her sleek hips and on the rondure of her thighs and on her long, slender, adolescent legs.

And yet, despite his obvious interest and her complete and total helplessness before him, he had never touched her, never laid hand upon her, never even tried to kiss her.

The only reason for this forebearance seemed to be the unknown force that drove Shamad on, night and day. He was filled with a strange tension, a restless urgent need to go ever onward. She was aware, from careless words he had let fall, and from bits of conversation between Shamad and his monsterling slave which she had overheard, that he well knew the boy warrior was close behind them, still on the trail of his revenge. But this alone was not enough to cause the fear and tension she saw in Shamad's every word and look and movement.

Zamog alone was more than a match for the young warrior of the Chayyim Kozanga, aye, and the old Easterling wizard, too. His dangling, apelike arms, swollen with massive thews, his broad, sloping shoulders, short bowed legs, and the immense barrel of his chest, naked save for a harness of belted straps, denoted strength and endurance that was far more than the human. Zamog could crush the life from the Nomad youth with a single hand!

It was not, then, the fear of the vengeance that pursued them and was ever at their heels, that drove the Impostor and his monstrous slave forward with such restless speed. It was something else, some sickness of the soul, perhaps. Or perchance it was, simply, that they had been running for so long that they could not pause or turn aside or double back, but could only continue running, as if impelled by a need that had by now become an unbreakable habit, a condition of life. It was strange; it was, somehow, horrible, this endless running away from something that followed close behind.

But then, the coldly beautiful man was—*mad*.

TIME BEGAN to blur together for Thyra. The hours became an endless procession of blurred sameness. They paused to rest or eat or sleep infrequently. The jarring ache in her bones, the bodily exhaustion that sapped her strength, the pain of her bound wrists, where tight thongs bit into her tender flesh, the chafed agony in her thighs caused by endless hours in the saddle, all of these dulled the edge of her consciousness. And the numb terror in her heart deadened her to any sense of time or place . . . they went ever onward, by night and by day, until it seemed at any moment they must come at last to the world's remote and ultimate Edge . . . and somehow a ghost of fear awoke within the numb, weary mind of the flamehaired girl at that thought . . . for it seemed to her that when they did arrive at the Edge the mad, restless demon of pursuit that dominated the broken mind of Shamad would urge him to goad them on and over the Edge of the World . . . and they should fall forever through the darkness of That Which Lay Beyond The World, the golden stars rushing past them in their endless fall . . . to fall forever through the limitless depths of the Universe . . . and Death itself would claim them before ever they reached whatever mystery was the Bottom of Infinity . . .

ON ACROSS the grey dunes they sped, and whether Lylix the sun star rode in the blue vault of heaven or whether the black dome of night was lit by many wandering and multicolored moons, the girl could not say.

And, after an eternity, they reached the Edge.

And there was nowhere else to go.

v. *Wings of Storm*

IT HAD been brewing all that day, and in the last hours before the sun star sank in a funeral pyre of crimson flame in the distant west, the storm struck at last.

They had known it was coming, the boy warrior and the old Easterling wizard. Thick clouds, black and turgid, swollen with vapors, had reared their dim castles against the sky since early afternoon. Within their tumultuous heart, the storm had been slowly engendered.

Now it spread its wings and struck at them.

Wind buffeted them and stinging sand blinded them, and viewless hands plucked and tore at their garments until Kadji could almost believe in Akthoob's tales of the ghosts of the dead who haunted these drear wastelands.

Gasping for breath, he sucked in dry sand and spat it out while fumbling with a bit of cloth to cover his eyes from the howling winds and the whirling grains of sand they bore on their mighty wings.

Beneath him, Haral stumbled and fell to his knees. Kadji slid down from the saddle and grabbed the reins, leading the little black Feridoon pony to where Akthoob stood. The old man had already dismounted and stood with his face pressed against the shoulder of his horse to keep the flying sand from his eyes.

"We can't ride in this murk," Kadji yelled in the old wizard's ear.

"This person agrees . . . yet we could be buried if we stand here like this," Akthoob shouted in hoarse reply.

"What can we do, then? There is no place wherein to take shelter from the storm—the land is as flat as the palm of my hand!"

At length, they decided to continue forward, but afoot, leading the horses. Muffling the heads of their steeds by winding cloth about them so as to protect eyes and ears and nostrils from the stinging blows of the howling sandstorm, and wrapping their cloaks about their own faces, the boy warrior and the old wizard led the horses forward, tugging at the reins. The grey wolf, Bazan, loped on ever ahead.

The journey seemed endless. The wind howled like a horde of demons and they were like to have smothered in the thick cloaks. Wind tore at them as they plodded forward, leaning into the blast, and their feet slipped and slid in the swirling sand underneath them. They had no idea where they were going, nor in which direction, and they dared not unveil their eyes in an attempt to tell their direction from the glow of the sun star. For sandstorms here in the Waste at the World's End can strike men blind: the winds that drive the stinging particles of sand have traveled far, and may perchance have begun on the surface of another world, blowing across the empty gulfs between this world of Gulzund and the next.

Thus they were plodding heavily along, heads downward, gasping for breath, feet slipping and sliding in the unsteady footing—when Zamog struck!

It was Haral saved the life of its young master. The Nomad youth, blinded and deafened by the storm, could not have seen the lurking Dragonman in time to defend himself. But the sharper senses of the little black pony scented the nearness of danger and of death. The pony halted suddenly, tossing its head, and neighed in a muffled cry. Then, as the blinded Kadji fumbled for the reins, the Feridoon pony reared, and struck out with sharp flying hooves whose blow would have smashed the skull of a man.

The hulking Dragonman had come out of the flying murk and was standing behind Kadji, lifting a gigantic scimitar. The monsterling had tracked the two humans and their horses for hours, ever since Shamad, arriving at the World's End and unable to go any farther, had sent him back to slay those who rode in pursuit. The lashing winds, the stinging sand, had bothered the giant Dragonman not the slightest. When the flying sand grains became painful, Zamog unsheathed the hard, transparent nictitating membranes within his eye-sockets and slid them across the scarlet eyes. Like all his monstrous kind, the Dragonman had no proper eyelids and slept with his eyes open.

The horse surprised him. He had not really noticed

the little black pony, his attention being fixed on the blinded, muffled Nomad boy. He had unwisely discounted the possibility of danger from the little black horse—very unwisely, as it turned out. For as Haral reared, the pony struck out with sharp hooves. Iron plates shod those hooves, and they were driven by the coiled and massive power of the horse's mighty shoulders, stronger and heavier than Zamog's own.

One caught him in the shoulder, half spinning him around. The other caught him full in the face.

Kadji slipped in the loose sand, trying to hold onto the reins of the bucking, kicking horse, and fell to his knees. Off balance, Zamog swung wildly but the scimitar whistled past Kadji and spun itself from the Dragonman's nerveless grip. The sledgehammer blow of the horse's hoof had broken his shoulder, and he would fight with that scimitar no more.

Kadji tore the cloth from his face and ripped the sacred Axe from the bosom of his robes and sprang at the staggering figure of Zamog, looming like some shambling demon of the storm amidst the flying murk.

But Haral's thundering hooves had won the fight. The second blow had taken the hapless monsterling full in the face. The force of a battering ram was behind that iron-shod hoof. The skull of a human being would have splattered like a broken egg shell before so terrific a blow. The tougher and heavier bone of the Dragonman's skull had held—but just barely.

Zamog lifted a mask of streaming horror to face the attack of the Nomad youth.

Both eyes were gone, smeared to liquescent ruin. The lower jaw was broken and hung and waggled helplessly, baring glistening and terrible fangs that could have torn Kadji's flesh to scarlet ruin if they could have closed on him. But they would never close again.

It was a marvel that the Dragonman lived. In fact, it

was a miracle that he was still on his feet. Staggering, blinded, one arm hanging like a dead weight from the shattered shoulder, the blue-scaled monsterling yet groped for the boy warrior with his single hand. Even then, had that hand closed on Kadji, such was the strength in that one good arm that it could have crushed the Red Hawk of the Chayyim Kozanga to mangled death.

But it did not.

The Axe of Thom-Ra lifted, glittering in the wan light of the dying sun star, and came flashing down.

The first stroke took Zamog full in the chest with a heavy *thunk* like a forester chopping wood. The glittering blade sank two inches into the tough, blue-scaled flesh: a rib or two cracked; Zamog staggered back, retaining his balance with some difficulty.

The second axe-blow took the Dragonman full on the side of the neck, half shearing off his head, and severing the spinal cord. It was a terrible wound: oily, malodorous serpent-gore pumped in a thick, gluey rope from a cut artery, slithering down his massive body to stain and besplatter the sands underfoot.

Zamog fell, slowly, in sections, like a tower whose foundations have eroded away. He went to his knees, then to all fours, then he sprawled at full length in the shifting sands. His broad, flat-tipped tail slapped the sand a time, then twitched spasmodically. And he died there in the cold grey sands at the World's Edge.

The sandstorm ended shortly thereafter, and the two mounted and rode forward again—due east.

170

vi. Before the Purple Gates

THYRA AWOKE slowly, as though from the spell of an interminable dream. For a long moment she merely lay there on the hard flat rock, half-wrapped in a torn cloak, blinking sleepily around her.

The towers of Ithombar, king city of the Immortals, rose directly before her. To incredible heights they soared, those slender, lofty spires. All of sparkling purple crystal were they built, and after a fashion unknown to mortal masons, for neither of block nor of brick were they composed, but of one fantastic mass of glittering glassy stuff, without seam or jointure. The imagination trembled and veered giddily away from picturing the furnaces in which those thousand-foot towers had been cast . . . *all in one piece.*

Directly before her rose the gates of the undying city wherein resided beyond death the mightiest and holiest of seers and saints, poets and philosophers—the great names and minds and hearts of this world of Gulzund, who had won their way to this place of perfect and unchanging peace one by one, over innumerable ages.

She stared at the mighty portals unbelievingly. Then, almost, she could have laughed. Poor Shamad! The last dream of conquest and empire was beyond even his lust to realize!

For the gates were . . . *locked.*

The rasp of boot-leather on dry gritty stone stung her to attentiveness. She turned her head around and froze, like one who wakes to find a deadly viper coiled within striking range.

She turned and saw Shamad the Impostor seated on a flat boulder not ten strides away. He squatted, tailor-fashion, and his strong, white hands played restlessly with a slender sharp knife. He was watching her, a faint smile on his face.

And suddenly she was very afraid.

Perhaps because fear took hold of her soul so completely, she stared at him, taking in very detail of his appearance. His raiment, once rich and kingly, was worn and stained and frayed to rags. The flesh had fallen from his powerful frame, leaving it mere bone and sinew and sun-dried flesh.

He was in need of a shave, his hollow, sunken cheeks shadowed by a growth of heavy stubble. His lips, which moved continuously, as if he whispered to someone she could not see, were colorless, dry and cracked. Small beads of foamy spittle glistened at the corners of his mouth.

His eyes burned feverishly in hollowed sockets, ringed with unhealthy circles. He looked ill; ill unto death.

His bright gaze shifted from her breasts to her face when he noticed that she was looking at him. He grinned, a rictus devoid of mirth, and spread lean hands in a gesture of self-mockery.

"Welcome to my throne room!" he said, laughingly. "My empire is somewhat smaller than it has been, and my court reduced in numbers to just you and me. Zamog"—he twitched his bony shoulders, and snatched a quick glance behind him—"has gone to slay the boy, your lover; but that was hours and hours ago; I fear even my loyal monsterling has left my service, like all the rest. Faithless, faithless! But I still have you," he said, his eyes returning to the girl suddenly.

Thyra was very afraid now. Her heart labored behind her ribs and her throat felt dry as dust. She sought to speak and coughed painfully.

"I have set wine beside you: drink, drink," he said tonelessly.

172

She drew one weak hand from under the cloak, found a cup, and drank deeply of the lukewarm, strong red wine. Eyes hooded, the Impostor watched her broodingly, slapping his dagger nervously against the rock with little dull ringing sounds.

Putting down the empty cup, she looked away from the ghastly expression on his face and stared up at the walls and gates of the silent, mysterious city. He followed the direction of her gaze, and his face contorted in a snarl.

"Locked, locked, locked, locked," he said harshly, then laughed, gesturing. "There is nowhere left for me to run!"

She followed his gesture and looked suddenly for the first time at the World's Edge.

As far as the eye could see in the harsh morning glare, a cliff of stone ran from horizon to horizon, cutting the sky in half. The desert waste simply stretched up to a point about thirty yards from where they were —and stopped. Beyond it there was only empty sky, blue, vacant, birdless. Not even a cloud was there to stain the purity of the azure infinity.

It was apalling. It was too vast to endure. The mind flinched away from it numbly, refusing to think of it. She averted her eyes from the terrific immensity—and found him staring at her.

"I understand why the boy, your lover, has followed me all this weary way . . ."

"He is not my lover! He has never touched me! I am a Virgin of Zoromesh and my Vows forbid me to—" she said hotly; he waved her words away with the hand that held the sharp knife.

"Words, words! You love him, do you not? And he, you?"

"Yes, I love Kadji, with all my heart and soul," she

173

said a trifle unsteadily. "As for him, I cannot say—never has he given me a look, a word—"

"Phaugh! You are children, children! He is sworn to a Quest of vengeance, to revenge the honor of his tribe —of course he is forbidden to the love of women, he cannot even speak a word of love, any more than can you!" Shamad said restlessly.

Breathlessly, Thyra looked at the madman with wide astonished eyes. Could it be so? Could that be why Kadji had seemed to rebuff her timid overtures back there in the cave months ago? It *must* be—what fools they both had been! Each sworn to chastity of body and of speech, by almost identical vows—and each not understanding the other was similarly bound!

". . . but why have you pursued me, girl? That is the one thing I have never understood. I have never harmed you," he said, almost plaintively. She steeled herself and looked him directly in the face: she was weak from endless hours of riding, so weak and exhausted she had swooned in the saddle; he could strike before she could untangle her limbs from the torn cloak and rise; but she spoke anyway. *Let it end here,* she thought.

"Have you forgotten how you dispatched your assassins to slay me—*me,* a Blood Princess of the House of Holy Azakour?"

He chewed on his lips thoughtfully, gazing at her with eyes a little sideways, eyes terribly bloodshot and weary.

"There is that, I suppose," he mumbled.

"But the real reason is that the sisterhood to which I belong has sent me hither to destroy you," she said, trying not to let her voice tremble. "For I am of the White Witches of Zoromesh, not yet a full sorceress, merely a girl of the novitiate; my mother pledged me to the sisterhood when I was but a child, and the Elder Sisters cared for me and sheltered me after she died."

A spark of interest flashed in his eyes.

"The White Witches? What have I ever done to offend them?" he cried, somewhat surprised by this revelation.

"You offend this earth of Gulzund by merely existing upon it," she said stoutly, drawing strength and courage from some unknown source within. "Your vile usurpation of the Holy Name and Throne of Yakthodah reeks to heaven and is an affront to the very Gods. They will not tolerate that one of baseborn blood besoil the Holy Dragon Throne! Thus was I sent to slay you if I could; if I could not, another would have followed me, and another . . ."

Suddenly Shamad leaped to his feet and sprang down from the flat-topped boulder and stalked over to her. His face was white and twitching as if something in her words had goaded him beyond all endurance.

"Then they had best unleash another witch on my track," he snarled. "For I shall slay you, aye, and that beardless boy that follows, and the old man, and that traitor Zamog, too, if still he lurks about—and then myself, I suppose."

Without another word he stooped and the sharp dagger blade flashed like a steel mirror in the fierce sun as he drove it at her breast—

vii. *World's End*

OUT OF NOWHERE a great grey wolf appeared. A shaggy, shadowy wolf, gigantic, fangs bared, growling thunderously. In his lean-muzzled face, eyes blazed like discs of golden flame.

He gathered himself, haunches tensing, hackles rising into a rough crest down his spine. Claws scratched and scrabbled on the naked rock as he seized a purchase and in the next instant launched himself into space like a grey thunderbolt.

Shamad had frozen in astonishment at the sudden appearance of the monstrous wolf. It was as if he had solidified out of blank nothingness like an apparition. So startled was he that he had involuntarily checked his knife blow and the blade's wicked point hovered above the flamehaired girl's breast.

Then the mighty wolf hurtled through the air and crashed into the stooping figure of the crazed Impostor. Fearsomely long, sharp fangs caught at the wrist of his knife hand; jaws crunched—bones snapped—blood spurted. Shamad shrieked, high and shrill like a child, as the jaws of the savage wolf closed on his hand.

The impact of the wolf's leap knocked the man flying. He fell on his back to the naked rock; the dagger spinning away to tinkle against stone.

The man shrieked again as he feebly tried to keep the snarling, snapping fangs from his face. The fetid, panting breath of the giant wolf was acrid and burningly hot on his face. In seconds his face and throat were slashed to ribbons and streaming with gore. He raised a face like a horrible scarlet mask, wherein only the mad, glaring eyes were still recognizable, in one heart rending glance at the frozen girl.

Then out of nowhere Kadji came, blocking out the sun, darkening the sky, face grim as vengeance itself.

In two great strides he was upon the struggling tangle of man and wolf. He bent, locked strong brown fingers in the ruff of fur at the wolf's shoulder and tore him away from the bubbling, shrieking thing.

The Axe of Thom-Ra lifted once, catching the sun, then fell in a mighty whistling stroke. The keen steel rasped and rang against naked rock. Blood squirted, startlingly scarlet, unbelievably beautiful pure color, in the sun.

And the severed head of Shamad rolled across the rocky floor to thud like an immense, soft, obscene fruit against the locked gates of the purple city.

Thus was the honor of the Chayyim Kozanga Nomads revenged.

Where all had been noise and motion and horror, now was a space of stillness. His battle fury calmed, the great wolf, Bazan, came padding over to where Thyra half lay, half crouched. The grey wolf whined deep in his throat and his long pink tongue came out to lick her cheek and the shaggy plume of his tail wagged furiously, for all the world like a great dog's.

"Well, that's done, bless us all!" sighed old Akthoob from somewhere in the background. Thyra laughed weakly.

Kadji bent and tore the throat of the corpse's garments open. The great gold medallion of the Dragon City lay against the naked breast of the headless thing. Thyra could have sworn the false corpse of the Emperor, which Shamad had left behind in the Khalidûr in his place while he fled in secret, hoping thus to delay pursuit, had worn the sacred emblem. But that must have been a forgery; Shamad could not bear to leave the ancient medallion of the Dragon behind and had worn it all this while.

Kadji removed the holy, precious thing and placed it within a deep pocket of his tunic. Then he bent and scrubbed clean the blade of the Axe of Thoma-Ra in the dry sand at the base of the flat boulder on which only a few minutes before the Impostor had squatted. Then he kissed the Axe which the War Prince of the Gods had given into the hands of his first ancestor many ages ago, and replaced the sacred weapon in his girdle.

Then while Thyra watched, he took up the headless corpse and bore it to the World's Edge. At his curt command, the old Easterling wizard gingerly took up the gory head of Shamad, holding it by a lock of hair, and carried it over to where Kadji stood on the brink of the Infinite.

The boy warrior raised the corpse above his head and then hurled it over the Edge of the World, even as old Akthoob, with a prim little expression of distaste, hurled the head after it. Over the World's Edge they fell, head and body, body and head, to fall forever and forever in the mocking gaze of the cold and watching stars.

Then the Nomad youth came over to where Thyra knelt and raised her in his strong arms. His handsome face, sunburnt, lean-jawed, serious, was very close to her own.

"How long were you there behind us?" she asked faintly.

"Long enough to hear that you loved me," he said. "Long enough to learn that you were bound by the same vows of chastity that sealed my lips against any expression of love. What fools we were, girl!"

"I have fulfilled my mission," she said dreamily. "Shamad is dead and the Gods are well pleased; the world is rid of him, and the Elder Sisters will be happy. I shall renounce my Vows; I have taken only the first of the Vows, the very little and unimportant Vows. Now I can speak of love: I love you, Kadji. Kadji!"

His eyes, clear, fearless, hawk-bright, stared into her own.

In a low voice he said: "And my Quest is done; the Axe of Thom-Ra has drunk deep of the blood of Shamad the Impostor, and the honor of my people is avenged! Thus have I fulfilled my own vow, and am released of its strictures. And now I, too, can speak of love. I love you, Thyra; I have loved you from the first moment I saw you there in the streets of Nabdoor-town, dressed in the gaudy finery of a Perushka wench. I have never loved any girl but you!"

The boy's arms tightened around her and they kissed, a long, deep, endless kiss. At last they drew apart a little, and the girl lay her head on the boy's shoulder and sighed a little, and laughed a little.

"What a strange place for us to meet, and to love at last," she said huskily. "Have lovers ever exchanged their vows here at the World's End?"

He smiled but did not answer, being content merely to stand and hold her close.

Behind them old Akthoob watched with twinkling eyes, a fond expression on his bony features.

"Ah!" he coughed. " 'Twas World's End for the false Shamad! For you twain, this humble person suggests it is not World's End but World's Beginning . . ."

The Epilogue

AFTER WORLD'S END

GOLDEN SUMMER had come back to the world of Gulzund again, and Kylix the sun star rode high in the son of her warm rays.

In the land of Maroosh, amidst the black mountains, where Chaya the Sacred River flows broad and strong from her secret source through the green and fertile valleys that lie forever locked away behind grim and impassive walls of unbroken stone, peace and plenty lay to every land.

The sword-brothers of the Chayyim Kozanga Nomads rested in the warmth, their wounds now healed, their decimated ranks replenished. Children ran and played along the curve of the great, slow-sweeping river; young lovers trysted in the reedy shallows where the heavy boughs of fruited *iongua* trees sheltered their whisperings and their doings from the eyes of the villagers; strong young warriors, stripped bare save for a rag twisted about their loins, stood thigh-deep in the clear waters, scrubbing down their stallions. Beyond the river, above the green meadow, where the cozy thatch-roofed huts nestled together in the flanks of the mountain wall, women ground corn in stone bowls, exchanged gossip as they scrubbed out their washing, or rested in the shadow of great trees while the noonday meal hissed deliciously over open-hearth fires.

In the stone-paved square before the House of the *jemadar*, Zarouk, Lord Chieftain of the Kozanga clans, stretched out his long legs and leaned back in the carven chair of ancient wood. About him a circle of fierce-eyed elders, hawk-nosed and white-bearded, disputed a troublous point of tradition. As for the tall chieftain, his wound now long-since healed, his strength long-since returned, he blinked and closed his eyes sleepily against the weight of golden sun and wished the hour of the midday feast had come.

IT WAS a keen-eyed sentinel, posted high in the crags above the secret valley where the warrior clans rested in peace and plenty, who spied them first: a yellow-haired boy mounted on a black Feridoon pony, a flamehaired girl of about the same age, riding a grey mare, with a great plains-wolf loping tirelessly at her side, and an old, lean-shanked Easterling, with bald pate and dangling queue, bouncing along on an ambling steed in the rear. The three strangers were winding their way through the tortuous maze that was the only pass through the black mountains, the pass that had been the closely guarded secret of the Chayyim Kozanga warriors since the far-off day of Kozang of Chaya himself, the first ancestor of the Nomad warrior clans.

His hand went to the great seven-foot-long warhorn bound with rings of pure brass, but he stayed his hand for a time, and bent again his keen gaze on the distant figures far below as they wound slowly through the black mountains toward the secret valley. Time enough to signal the approach of enemies; one more long look he would take, for there was something familiar about that yellow-haired boy, something about the way he sat his steed, something in the set of his shoulders, and the way one brown hand clenched the reins, bending up a little from the wrist . . . true, the bright-haired boy was a boy no longer, but nigh unto manhood, fleshed out and broader of shoulder, stronger of back, more powerful of arm than he remembered . . . but something about the strong, sunburnt youth reminded him of . . . of . . . could it be? . . .

THEY REINED to a halt before the last turning of the pass, and Kadji reached out and took the hand of his wife in his own and smiled into her smiling face. In a moment or two they would ride on, down into the valley, the ancient homeland of his people, the cradle of his race, into the strong arms of his Grandfather and into the thunderous, triumphant welcome of the sword-brothers . . . but in a moment: not now; not quite yet.

In five months they had come all the way back across the wide-wayed world to where his Quest had begun a year or more before. But the road back had been easier than the hard long road to World's End. They had struck south from the gates of Ithombar, and, in easy stages, had reached the Easterling port city of Naranga-zaya, and the great ships, and the mysterious seas of the south.

There, what little was left of their gold had purchased a slow, lazy voyage for them, from isle to isle, from sea to sea, all along the coast of the world until at last they had come ashore south of the Great Plains, horses and all, for the last ride north into the land of Maroosh where the impassable ring of the black mountains guarded forever the secret valley of the Chayyim Ko-zanga from a thousand enemies.

Aboard the fat-bellied merchant ship they had hired
—the *Arthayan Queen* she was called, and her captain
a fat, sleepy old rogue of an Easterling who had passed
the months of the voyage playing an inscrutable and
mysterious board-game with old Akthoob, something
involving multicolored polygons and tiny carven ivory
pieces, Kadji could never puzzle it out—had come a
black-robed priest of All Gods, bound for the High
Temple at jungled Thash. He had married the boy
Kadji and the girl Thyra there on the deck of the *Arthayan Queen*, in the presence of all the crew, one magni-
ficient night with seven moons aloft to light the heavens
in honor of their nuptials.

That was many months ago; and as he stood there,
holding the hand of the flamehaired girl he had followed
across the very world to its ultimate and terrible Edge,
Kadji smiled, thinking of the son she bore within her at
this moment. For old Akthoob had peered into the
mists of unborn tomorrows and had emerged smiling
and bobbing and promising a strong son with the clear,
fearless blue eyes of his father and the gorgeous flamegold mane of his royal mother. . . .

One day, perhaps, they would come thundering out
of the black mountains, the mighty host of the Chayyim
Kozanga, to win that flamehaired and yet unborn lad's
birthright for him at the point of a thousand swords;
aye, one day . . . for a blood-feud yet stood between the
Kozanga and the dog-knights of Rashemba, and whether it was the High Prince Bayazin or some high and
mighty lordling of the *kugars* who had been victorious
in the civil war that had wracked golden Khôr when
Kadji fled from it a year ago on the track of Shamad the
Impostor, and who now clung precariously to his
unsteady place upon the Dragon Throne, it mattered little, for both were foemen of the Chayyim Kozanga!

The heart of the young warrior quickened at the

thought of it, but it was only just and true: his wife, Thyra, was the last living survivor of the House of the Holy Azakour, and the son of her blood and his had a claim to the Dragon Empire stronger than that of any man or woman yet alive on Gulzund. And mayhap someday, with a thousand Kozanga war banners rustling over her head, Thyra would ride with Kadji and the boy and old Grandfather, too, across the whispering plains to the gates of the Dragon City, to claim rightful heritage. And thus the Chayyim Kozanga would weld their fighting strength to the ancient royal power and wealth of the Dragon Throne, and from this mingling would arise an Empire mightier than any that had ever risen aforetime, such as would stand forever and ever until at last the sun burnt out and the world went dark and cold . . . ah, it was a lovely dream! And it yet might all come true. . . .

Behind him, old Akthoob was grumbling loudly, saying something about the midday meal, and Haral, the black Feridoon pony, snuffing in the old, familiar scent of the green meadows of the Chaya's banks, the warm sweet smells of home, was nickering eagerly.

And then, from far above, from high among the towering crags, a great wondering cry rang out—at which, beyond the curve, in the sunlit village, Zarouk the old *jemadar* started to his feet, his heart a fountain of glorious joy, his eyes brimming with glad tears, and at the sound of which all of the great sword-brothers sprang to their feet, snatching up sword and buckler to crash steel against steel in the iron song of welcome.

From far above their heads the great, joyous cry rang out: *"Hail, Kozanga! . . . Kadji . . . Kadji . . . Kadji! . . . Cry welcome and hail, for the Red Hawk of the Chayyim Kozanga returns . . . and lo! he has become a man in his travels . . . O, Kadji . . . Kadji, . . . Kadji . . . !"*

And he laughed and squeezed the girl's hand and

grinned at the old Easterling wizard and nudged the little black Feridoon pony forward, and they rode around the curve, and they were home. The Quest of Kadji was ended.

don't stop reading

If you have read as far as this,
you'll realise why Five Star
Paperbacks are among the
best. And there's plenty
more to choose from.

A complete list of titles
in this series for your
enjoyment

Westerns

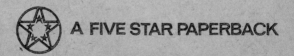 **A FIVE STAR PAPERBACK**

A complete list of titles
in this series for your
enjoyment

Thrillers

THE CELLAR BOYS
H. Baker
THE LAST LAUGH
P. Denver
BENNY MUSCLES IN
Peter Rabe
TAKE A STEP TO MURDER
D. Keene
MURDER AT THE MOTEL
Victor Gun
THE OUT IS DEATH
P. Rabe
DANGER FOR BREAKFAST
J. McPartland
DEATH AT TRAITORS GATE
Victor Gunn
CALAMITY CONQUEST
Berkeley Gray
THE SCRAMBLED YEGGS
R. S. Prather
BODIES IN BEDLAM
R. S. Prather
DIE LIKE A MAN
M. Delving

Occult Thrillers

THE QUEST OF KADJI
Lin Carter
THE WIDDERBURN HORROR
R. Warner-Crozetti
THE BLACK DOG
Georgena Goff
DEVIL SOUL
Victor Jay
WIZARD OF STORMS
Dave Van Arnam

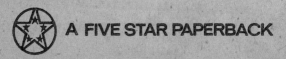 **A FIVE STAR PAPERBACK**

A complete list of titles
in this series for your
enjoyment

Romances

LAMENT FOR JULIE
R. Colby

BEAUTIFUL BUT BAD
R. Colby

KIM
R. Colby

ANDREA HOLLAND
B. Frame

A TIME FOR STRENGTH
N. M. Dean

THIS GIRL
J. Hytes

THAT FRENCH GIRL
Joseph Hilton

Gothic Romances

THE HOUSE ON SKYHIGH ROAD
I. S. Way

TERROR AT DEEPCLIFFE
D. Nile

THE DEADLY ROSE
K. Rich

MISTRESS OF THE SHADOWS
R. McLeod

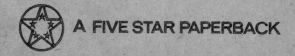 A FIVE STAR PAPERBACK